TAKE HOLD OF TOMORROW

Determined for a better future, Ellen, a kitchen maid, takes every opportunity to further herself and is promoted to lady's maid. But the advancement in her status attracts declarations of love from three very different men: John, the master's son; Charlie, a farmer's lad; and Leslie, her mistress's fiancé. Jealousy and betrayal plague her life once more and grasping hold of a better tomorrow is a dream that is beginning to slip away.

TAKE HOLD OF TOMORROW

TAKE HOLD OF TOMORROW

by

Karen Abbott

Magna Large Print Books
Long Preston, North Yorkshire,
BD23 4ND, England.

British Library Cataloguing in Publication Data.

Abbott, Karen
    Take hold of tomorrow.

    A catalogue record of this book is
    available from the British Library

    ISBN   978-0-7505-3866-4

First published in Great Britain in 2013 by Robert Hale Limited

Copyright © Karen Abbott 2013

Cover illustration © Collaboration JS by arrangement with
Robert Hale

The right of Karen Abbott to be identified as the author of this
work has been asserted by her in accordance with the
Copyright, Designs and Patents Act, 1988

Published in Large Print 2014 by arrangement with
Robert Hale Ltd.

Magna Large Print is an imprint of Library Magna Books Ltd.

Printed and bound in Great Britain by
T.J. (International) Ltd., Cornwall, PL28 8RW

I dedicate *Take Hold of Tomorrow* to my two
grandmothers: Elsie May Mitchell and
Ellen Ridings, parts of whose lives
influenced the writing of this novel;
and to all my friends in Horwich
who love to read about 'our' town.

One

1900

It was time to go.

Ellen Durban's stomach lurched. Her throat hurt and she felt sick, but she couldn't, for shame, say so. She didn't want them to think she was a softie. Besides, she was almost eleven years old and was too big to cry, even though she had been taken from her home and family and moved far away from the smoke-filled streets of Miles Platting on the outskirts of Manchester. Now she was in a town called Horwich, a town she hadn't even heard of until two days ago.

They'd travelled by train; a great big iron monster that hissed out steam and black smoke as it rattled and jolted its way out of the city, past the countless ends of blackened terraced houses and factories all the way to Bolton; and then on another train that was soon passing through lovely green fields, a sight that had quite taken her breath away. She'd never seen a green field before, except in picture books at school.

She'd seen trains, of course. Who hadn't, living where they did? Trains rattled by all day long, making the houses and other buildings shake and rattle in unison. She had learned yesterday that the trains used to be built in Miles Platting until the managers of the Lancashire and Yorkshire railway works decided that they needed to expand the repair shop – and, since the city had grown around and beyond the railway works, they looked elsewhere for a suitable tract of land. They found it in Horwich, a small town that nestled under the southern end of the Pennines.

They moved everything, lock, stock and barrel, including many of the railway workers – them as wanted to go, that is – and who wouldn't? It was good money. Even her own grandparents had gone, which was why she had never met them until two days ago.

Her granny – or 'Grandma', as she had been told to call her – said the town wasn't so small now, though it seemed small to Ellen. Why, they'd not long left Panton Street, where Grandma and Grandpa lived, and were now walking along Chorley New Road towards Bolton – and they had already left the town behind them!

And then, when it seemed there were only green fields ahead, they turned left up Ainsworth Avenue by a big house called 'Swallowfields'. For a moment, Ellen thought that was where she was going to work and her heart missed a beat. It looked lovely – but so grand. Why, she'd bet even old Queen Victoria wouldn't mind living there! They'd need a lot of servants, though – which was what she was going to be. Kitchen maid, Grandma said, for the Oldfield family who owned a nearby brickworks.

Grandma and Grandpa were carrying a wooden box, each holding one of its rope handles. It was for Ellen to keep her belongings in. Not that she had much. Her school frock was in there, just in case she needed it, and from the market, Grandma had got her some nearly new underwear, some stockings and two grey frocks, one of which she was wearing now. As Grandma had pinned up the hem to the right length, she had promised to help Ellen learn how to make more for herself later on, and to teach her other things that would help her get on. 'Your mother tells me you have the ability, Ellen,' she had said. 'It's up to you to do your best.'

Ellen nodded. Her mam used to say, 'Yer not going in t'mill, our Ellen! Yer can do better than that!'

When the rest of her friends had left school, she'd heard her mam and stepfather yelling at each other about it and, although her mam had been covered in bruises the following day, she'd been allowed to stay on at school since September, helping with the little ones, hoping to eventually become an assistant teacher – but that dream had now been shattered. There'd be no more school for her.

Ellen pulled her shawl a little tighter. It had been Mam's shawl; she had given it to her as she left home. 'It'll help you remember me,' she'd whispered. As if she'd ever forget her mam! She loved her mam. It was that man she hated!

They were still going higher up the road, past the brickworks that Mr Oldfield owned, and a few more houses; and then just green fields. The higher they trudged, the fresher and cleaner the air tasted. Ellen wished she could put some of it in a bottle and send it home to her mam. It'd help to clear that nasty cough she had.

When they reached the brow of the rise, there was a range of hills in the near distance. She'd seen them yesterday when she had gone with Grandma into town to get her a pair of boots. They were a bit big for her but Grandma said she'd grow into them before the year was over. They'd stuffed a bit of paper into the toes to help them stay on her feet.

She wished her best friend Mary could see her new boots. She'd be quite envious – and they wouldn't half give Jimmy Clarke, who lived further down their street, a good kick on his shins the next time he pulled her hair! Except she wouldn't be there any more to be tormented by him, would she?

A feeling of sadness washed over her. She'd even put up with Jimmy Clarke chanting rude rhymes at her, if it meant she could go home.

But she couldn't.

It wasn't fair. She'd done nowt wrong. It was him, her stepfather. It was all his fault!

'See that highest hill, Ellen?'

Grandpa's voice broke into her thoughts and she looked in the direction he was pointing. The highest hill, the one right at the south-western end, had a small tower on top of it.

'That's Rivington Pike,' Grandpa told her. 'And look, over there. That's called Rockhaven Castle.'

True enough, a square-built castle stood on the skyline.

'Can I go and see it?'

'Don't go filling her head with fantasy, Abram,' Grandma snapped. 'She's here to work. She won't be having much time to admire her surroundings. A half-day off every other Sunday is what she'll get, if she's lucky. Besides, it's not a real castle. It's just a big house made to look like one.'

'Gosh!' Ellen was impressed. 'Fancy having enough money to do that!'

Grandma sniffed. 'More money than sense, some folks.'

Ellen's shoulders slumped. The spark of interest died away. Her legs ached and her feet were hurting. Her footsteps dragged.

'Walk properly, Ellen!' her grandma admonished sharply. 'You'll ruin your new boots! You're old enough to know better!'

Old enough to leave school. Old enough to earn her keep. Old enough for ... other things, Ellen thought bitterly. Her chest tightened and tears threatened to fill her eyes.

'We're almost there,' Grandpa broke in. 'Look.' He pointed ahead to a house surrounded by a high stone wall. It was so high Ellen could only see the top floor of the house over it. 'The gate's just along there. Go on. Go and have a look.'

She ran ahead and stopped in front of the

pair of wrought-iron gates set between two stone pillars. It was a plain house, built of stone. Ellen's stomach tightened. She felt scared. This was where she was going to live; and she didn't know anyone. She could feel her lips trembling.

Abram Hilton stood beside her. He put his hand on her shoulder. 'That's the house, Ellen. What do you think of it?'

Ellen flinched at his touch and stepped aside. The house stood about twenty yards back from the wall. It looked cold; not nice and friendly like that house at the bottom of the road. Large windows almost filled up the lower level of the house. And, by golly, they shone like ... like... She couldn't think of anything that shone so brightly, except maybe heaven.

The front garden was nice, though. It had a lawn in front of the house and a wide, cobbled driveway that led to some rounded stone steps that rose up to the front door. There were flower beds full of shrubs and some lovely flowers. And then a high stone wall that stretched out at both sides of the house.

Ellen let out a sigh. 'The garden's beautiful.' Maybe it wouldn't be so bad working here. She'd be able to play in the garden and pick some of those lovely flowers and, who knew, maybe even take some home to her mam one day!

Dorcas forced a smile. 'This is the nearest you'll get to all of this, Ellen. I'm afraid your entrance is around at the back. Come on, Abram. Let's get on.'

Abram and Dorcas picked up the handles of the box again and Ellen followed them alongside the front wall until they reached its far end. Here, they turned, with the wall on their left-hand side, and followed it as far as a wooden gateway.

As Grandpa pressed the latch, the gate swung open, Ellen could see a cobbled yard with a number of outbuildings to the left and right, each with a small window and a wooden door that was fastened and bolted, hiding their contents and uses.

She followed her grandparents through the gate. As they neared the end of the right-hand side row of outbuildings, the rear garden came into view. A thick hedge seemed to run the entire length of it, starting from the middle of the rear house-wall and cutting the garden in half. What was on the other side of the hedge was not to be seen from this position, except the top of a tall tree, but on this side there were a number of regimented

16

flower beds, where some summer flowers were blooming in splendour; beyond them were rows and rows of vegetable beds. Some plants with no flowers grew at the edges of the soil, whilst in the far distance were a few trees bearing small apples and pears. At the extreme right-hand side stood a glasshouse and a number of cold frames.

Suddenly, the unaccustomed grandeur was too much and Ellen felt physically sick. It was too big; too grand; too far from home! How was she going to bear it? She wanted her mam or their Tom.

Abram and Dorcas halted a few feet from the large kitchen door. This was as far as they were to accompany her. Ellen looked up at them, not trusting herself to speak.

Grandpa lightly touched her cheek and she tried not to flinch away. His voice was kind though; not like Zach Durban's. 'Head high, Ellen. You've got what it takes.'

Grandma spoke more sharply in her farewell. 'We'll meet you after morning service at church a week next Sunday, Ellen. Work hard, and then they will be pleased with you. And don't forget to say your prayers before you go to sleep.' She bent stiffly down and planted a kiss on her granddaughter's cheek, then hurried away without a backward glance, clutching her husband's arm.

Ellen watched until they reached the gateway. Grandpa turned and raised his hand in salute. Then they were gone from sight.

Forcing back threatening tears, Ellen turned around and knocked timidly on the plain wooden door, holding her breath as the door was pulled open. A round-faced girl stood there, staring at her as if uncertain how to proceed.

'Who is it, Doris?' a voice called from inside the kitchen.

'I dunno, Cook. I've never seen her before.'

'Then ask her who she is and what she wants!'

'Who are you and what d'you want?' Doris obediently repeated.

'Er ... I'm t'new kitchen maid,' Ellen squeezed through her dry throat.

'She's the new kitchen maid,' Doris called over her shoulder.

'Yes, we heard! Well, tell her to come in, then!'

'You'd best come in,' Doris invited, standing back to allow Ellen to step inside.

Quelling her nervousness, Ellen stepped over the threshold and stared around. By heck, it was big! Far bigger than their kitchen-cum-living room at home! Bigger than their whole house, she was sure. Her wide eyes moved slowly around the room, taking in the huge, black-leaded open-range fire, with an enormous oven at the side; rows of gleaming copper pans hanging from the holes in their handles, carefully graded from the largest to the smallest; the large dresser standing against the opposite wall, its shelves holding a variety of plates, dishes, large soup tureens and an assortment of different-sized jugs. Cupboards surrounded the whole room, some standing on the floor and some fixed to the wall, between which a variety of kitchen tools were hanging; yet more tools were hanging from the ceiling.

A knotted rope held a wooden clothes rack in its raised place above the kitchen range, with a mixture of cloths suspended from it, drying in the heat from the burning coals. Two large, stone sinks filled the space at the end of the kitchen, each with a long wooden draining board; and in the middle of the kitchen stood a large, well-scrubbed wooden table where five people were seated.

Ellen suddenly realized that all five faces were turned towards her. Her cheeks burned with embarrassment.

'Is she gormless, or what?' a girl with blonde hair inquired of everyone.

19

Ellen flushed even deeper but she managed to smile nervously. The girl, quite striking in appearance, was seated at the foot of the table. She looked about sixteen years old. Her blonde hair, teased into curls, framed her face around the edges of her cap. She was quite pretty, though she had a hard, calculating look in her eyes. She wore a plain black frock and had a small, plain white cap on her head.

The one called Doris had scuttled across the kitchen and seated herself beside the blonde girl. She was dressed as she herself was, in a plain grey frock, with all of her hair tucked up inside a large white mobcap, gathered around its edge.

'Well, come in if you're stopping, girl!' It was a severe-faced man, seated at the head of the table, who had spoken.

Ellen looked at him warily. Dressed in black trousers, black waistcoat and white shirt, he looked as though he might be in charge. Her eyes narrowed slightly; then she cast them down, not wanting him to see her aversion to his presence. At his side was a large woman, whose dark grey hair was twisted neatly into a large bun and was topped by a small lace cap. Her face was red and shiny and, although she was looking at her quite sternly,

Ellen didn't feel too alarmed by her.

Opposite her was a pleasant-faced young woman, neatly dressed in a fitted black frock, with a small frilled white apron over it and a white cap on her dark hair, which was also neatly fashioned in a bun. Her lips formed a friendly smile.

Ellen smiled back a bit uncertainly, thankful for a friendly face.

'Well, sit yourself down, then,' the large woman commanded impatiently. 'We haven't got all day!'

'Yes, ma'am. I mean, no, ma'am,' Ellen stammered, still feeling overawed by the set of faces watching her.

The golden-haired girl chortled. 'Did you hear that? "Yes, ma'am. No, ma'am. Three bags full, ma'am!"'

Ellen flushed under the older girl's mocking scorn.

'Give over, Goldie,' the older woman said sharply, 'and I'm not "ma'am", girl. I'm Mrs Garland, the cook. Address me by my name or title, as you please. Take a seat and help yourself to some bread an' jam if you're hungry.'

Ellen slid onto one of the vacant chairs opposite Doris. Doris gave her a flicker of a smile but cut it off abruptly after an anxious

21

look at Goldie.

'What do we call you, then?' asked the pleasant-faced young woman.

Ellen blushed again. Her throat felt like grit, as she swallowed hard. 'Me name's Ellen Dur–' No! She wasn't going to use that name ever again. Her real dad had been called Harris. Tom Harris, her mam had said. That would be her name now. She cleared her throat. 'Harris, ma – Cook. Ellen Harris,' she repeated more firmly.

'Well, I hope you're a good worker, Ellen. We don't carry no passengers here. Doris, get Ellen a cap and apron out of the linen cupboard.'

'Let's get the introductions over with and then we can get on with our meal,' the man at the top of the table said. He held his knife and fork still for a moment and then waggled the knife in Ellen's direction. 'I'm the master's valet, butler and footman. Cadman upstairs, Bert down here. Mrs Garland, housekeeper-cum-cook, you've already met; and Nora Tucker, parlourmaid, chamber-maid, lady's maid. We all have a few jobs here.'

He pointed his knife at Goldie. 'That's Janet Goulding, known as Goldie down here, and the other's Doris. She's just Doris, 'cos she never works upstairs. Goldie works for Nora upstairs and Cook downstairs.' He paused to wag his knife at her. 'You and Doris are scullery maids, kitchen maids, anybody's maids. The only time that's your own is when you've gone to bed; and you only go there when one of us three have given you leave. Got that?'

Cook and Nora nodded at his summing up of their positions. Goldie tilted her head arrogantly. 'And I'm senior to you. So you'd better do as I tell you and be quick about it! We don't have no lazybones down here, do we, Doris?'

Doris vigorously nodded her head, changing it to a shake when Goldie frowned. 'That's right,' she agreed. 'We've to do as Cook or Nora tells us.'

'In short,' Bert continued, 'you are last in the pecking order. Well, next to last. By the look of you, you'll soon be in front of Doris. You may as well get used to it, because it will be a long time before it changes.' He indicated the breadboard with his knife and Nora pushed it along the table towards Ellen. 'Help yourself. It's your last till morning.'

The board held the remains of a freshly baked loaf. A dish of butter and a pot of jam were within reach. In spite of the butterflies still swirling around inside her, Ellen's eyes gleamed. Best butter and jam – together! Maybe it wasn't going to be too bad here!

Once the meal was over, the three older ones pushed back their chairs.

Cook took command. 'Doris, show Ellen where the outside lavvy is and then come with me to the cold store. When you come back in, Ellen, you can clear this table and get everything washed and dried. Nora, you know what you've to do. Goldie, get the cream from the dairy, and then go with Bert to prepare the dining room.'

There was barely time to breathe in the next two hours as they prepared, served and cleared away the family's Sunday high tea and when that was over, the orders began again.

'Come on, Ellen. There's all the under-wear to be put to soak, ready for tomorrow.' Nora already had her arms full of dirty linen. 'Pick that other lot up and follow me outside into the yard. We'll just be able to see what we're doing.'

In one of the outhouses, Nora dumped the clothes into a huge stone sink filled with water. 'Now go back in for the kitchen cloths. You'll find them in a pile under the table. We get the bed linen in the morning.'

The jobs seemed endless and it was a great relief when Ellen realized that Mrs Garland was satisfied that all that needed to be done had indeed been done.

'Finish what you're doing, Doris, then you can take Ellen upstairs and get the pair of you to bed. It's an early start in the morning. Don't be late. Be down here at five o'clock, prompt. D'you hear?'

Their beds were in two small, square rooms, up four flights of plain wooden stairs, right at the top of the house; Nora and Goldie in one, Doris and Ellen in its twin on the opposite side of the steep wooden stairs. The only window was a square of glass in the roof. The ceiling sloped down on one side. They were obviously up in the attic. Ellen shivered. It felt quite cold up there after the warmth of the kitchen.

The light from the candle Doris carried added to the thin shaft of moonlight shining in through the small fanlight. There was a bed, placed up against the wall on the left-hand side of the room, and a small cupboard against the wall under the fanlight. Her box was there, too. Bert must have carried it up for her whilst she was helping Nora.

'I'm sleeping by the wall,' Doris said, 'then

25

you can't push me out of bed. You're on the edge. Goldie liked it that way. She used to share with me but she's had to move in with Nora. She said I could make you sleep by the wall if I wanted but I don't want you crawling all over me if you get out for a pee in the night. The po's under the bed. You have to empty it!' She put the candle on the cupboard, took off her apron and frock and dropped them onto the floor. Then she crawled across to the far side of the bed. 'Blow the candle out when you're ready.'

Ellen undressed and laid her folded clothes neatly on the bedrail at the end of the bed. Then she blew out the candle and lay down on the edge of the bed. It was a long time since she had had to share a bed with either of her sisters. Her nose wrinkled at the sweaty smell that came from Doris's body and she turned away onto her side.

She must have fallen asleep, though she had no recollection of doing so, and she wasn't fully aware that she had woken. A vision of her stepfather had suddenly filled her mind; his sweaty body; the stale smell of ale and tobacco, mixed with the pungent aroma of the pickled onions he treated himself to as he propped up the bar at the local ale house; his rotting teeth; and his chin that

26

felt as rough as a yard brush as he pounded himself into her rigid body.

With a sharp cry, she forced herself fully awake. Her eyes tried to pierce the darkness. Where was she? Where was the street lamp? Its flickering light usually glowed through the tattered curtains. It was never as dark as this.

A throaty snore at her side sent her scrabbling wildly towards the foot of the bed. He was in bed with her! He'd be at her again! She wouldn't let him! She wouldn't! She'd–

'Give over, Ellen! What the 'eck d'you think you're doin'?'

Doris's plaintive tones puzzled her for a moment. She froze, her ears alert, waiting.

'Ellen? Give us back me covers. It's freezing. Get back to sleep, will yer.'

It was Doris; not Zach. She was far away from him. She was safe. She slowly relaxed and crawled back under the bedclothes, curling her body into a tight ball. The tears that she had refused to shed in public now burned hot and seeped out of her tightly closed lids, running over the bridge of her nose and down her other cheek into the lumpy pillow.

She wanted her mam; and Tom and Jack, and Flossie and Maud, her brothers and sisters, and Herbie, the baby. Were they missing her?

Or had they forgotten her already?

Two

They were wakened in the morning by Mrs Garland knocking on her ceiling with a brush handle. Ellen shivered. It was dark and cold. She wished she could go back to sleep. She still felt tired but the memory of her nightmare made her eager to leave the attic bedroom. She slid off the bed and groped around for her clothes, pulling them on as fast as she was able.

Doris was doing likewise. 'Don't forget to put your cap on,' she reminded Ellen.

There wasn't time to brush out her plait and redo it. Ellen retied its ribbon and pushed it up inside the plain mobcap she'd been given and stumbled after Doris down the wooden stairs. The other servants were already in the kitchen, bustling about. Two bowls of porridge sat side by side on the table. Ellen looked at them longingly.

'You're late!' Cook snapped. 'I hope you're

not going to make a habit of it. Ellen, put this bit of sacking over your pinny and take over raking out the grate, then Goldie can go up and get the fire grates done on the ground floor. Doris, go and get another bucket of coal. You can have your porridge when you've done that.'

Goldie smirked as she stood up and pulled Ellen's cap down over her eyes. 'Jump to it, lazybones, or I'll make sure you don't last the week out!'

Ellen straightened her cap, scowling at the girl, but she crouched down at the grate and took over raking through the cinders. She was used to doing this at home – but, by golly, what a rush everything was! By the time she had cleaned the grate and set the fire, there was just time to eat the bowl of porridge and then she and Doris went out to the wash house to light the boiler in there to get the water heated up. Whilst it was heating, they checked the clothing that had been soaking overnight for stains and rubbed them with lye soap against the scrubbing-board. Ellen's knuckles were red raw by the time they were putting the first lot of clothing into the dolly tub, where the clothes were pounded with the dolly stick to loosen the rest of any soiling. Then they had to haul everything into the heated water in the copper boiler to be boiled for an hour with more lye soap to get them properly clean ... whilst they started on the next lot.

'We can go in for some toast now,' Doris said.

Ellen was glad of the break. Her arms were aching but there was no time to dawdle. Nora was sending the family's breakfast dishes down the serving shaft and Goldie was piling them by one of the sinks, ready to be washed. Mrs Garland was deftly turning over some rashers of bacon in the frying pan. The appetizing smell made Ellen's mouth water.

'Grab yourselves a piece of toast,' Cook said over her shoulder, 'and wash them dishes. Then you can have a piece of this bacon before you go back to the wash house.'

As Ellen reached out for a piece of toast, a sudden hush fell over the kitchen. She was surprised to see Doris hurriedly slide out of her seat and stand to attention. She realized that Mrs Garland and Goldie had performed the same act.

A pair of delicately covered ankles and a pale blue skirt were descending the short flight of steps that led out of the kitchen.

'Ellen!' Doris hissed, making frantic beckoning movements.

Ellen glanced from the almost complete figure to the kitchen maid. What was happening? She put down her toast and slid off her chair, joining Doris at the end of the table. Doris tugged at her dress. 'It's Mrs Oldfield,' she hissed. 'You've to curtsey.'

Ellen dropped into a belated curtsey, raising her eyes to see the tall, slender woman, dressed in a plain but well-cut gown, bearing down upon her.

'What's your name, girl?' Mrs Oldfield demanded.

'Ellen, Mrs ... er...' Ellen stammered. Her neck seemed to be locked in its backwards tilt.

Mrs Oldfield's eyes narrowed. 'Ellen what?'

'Ellen Harris.' She said it slightly defiantly, wondering if her employer expected her to be using her stepfather's name.

Mrs Oldfield's hand shot out, slapping the side of Ellen's face, sending her staggering into Doris. 'Don't you dare speak to me in that tone of voice! Didn't your mother teach you any manners?'

Ellen recovered her balance and nodded, her eyes bright with unshed tears. 'Yes. Only I–' Her lips wouldn't form the right words.

'Don't answer back, girl, except to say, "Yes, ma'am" or "No, ma'am"! And curtsey before you speak. Is that understood?'

Ellen nodded dumbly. She risked lifting her head a little and saw Mrs Garland standing behind their employer, mouthing, 'Yes, ma'am', at her.

She gulped. 'Yes, ma'am.'

'Good. You will be called Harris here. And get a clean cap on your head! It looks as though you have cleaned the floor with it!'

Ellen raised her hands to remove the offending cap, her eyes narrowing at the sooty handprint on it. Goldie had done that!

Before she knew what was happening, Mrs Oldfield had snatched hold of her plait, dragging her forward.

'Ouch!' Her instinctive resistance pulled the end of her plait out of her employer's hand, leaving behind the scrap of ribbon that had bound its end. Her chestnut curls immediately began to spring apart.

Mrs Oldfield drew in her breath. 'You look as though you have been dragged through a hedge! I will not have slovenly servants in my house. If you cannot look after your own hair, girl, you must have it cut off! Mrs Garland, see to it before the day is out!'

Ellen put her hands to her head, covering as much hair as she could. 'No! I can look after it! Only there wasn't time!'

'Precisely. See to it, Mrs Garland.'

Mrs Oldfield's eyes swept around the kitchen. Her eyebrows rose in disdain. 'You asked for extra staff in here, Mrs Garland, but I really can't see the benefit.'

Mrs Garland curtseyed again, her heart all a-flutter, she later confessed to Nora. 'Harris only started this morning, ma'am. She hasn't had chance to learn what to do yet.'

'I don't pay people to learn their job, Mrs Garland. I expect them to be able to do it!' Her attention swung back to Ellen. 'I give you one week, without pay, to learn your job, Harris. If the work is too much for you, you will have to go. Is that clear?'

Ellen nodded, unable to speak.

'Is that clear?'

Ellen swallowed hard. She had to be able to stay. She couldn't go back home. 'Yes, ma'am,' she whispered.

'Good!' As Mrs Oldfield turned to go, she gestured with her hand towards the remains of the toast and mugs of tea on the table. 'Get all of that cleared away at once, Mrs Garland.'

'Yes, ma'am.'

Silence remained until the latch on the door at the top of the stairs was heard to click into place. Then Mrs Garland leapt into action.

'You heard what she said. Get that lot cleared away and get the pair of you out to the wash house. We'll deal with your hair later, Ellen. Goldie, go and help Nora upstairs and then join this pair outside. Come on! Get on with it!'

Goldie's face was covered in a wide grin. Ellen longed to wipe it from her face with a scathing remark but had the sense to know this wasn't the time. She stuck her chin in the air and followed Doris out of the kitchen with as much dignity as she could muster.

There wasn't time for moping. The work was non-stop. The rest of the clothes needed to be sorted and then pounded with the three-legged dolly. By which time, the previous load needed to be mangled, rinsed in three lots of water, mangled again and then hung out to dry.

Goldie came to help with that, as the clothes line was too high for Ellen and Doris. Ellen kept a wary eye on her and was glad when she returned inside without having caused more trouble. Her relief was short-lived. When Goldie came out again a few minutes later, she was brandishing a pair of scissors.

'Haircut time!' she grinned.

Ellen clutched hold of both sides of her cap and backed away. 'Oh no, you don't! I'd rather Nora did it.'

'Get hold of her, Doris!' Goldie snapped. 'Mrs Garland says I've got to cut it now because Mrs Oldfield's coming down to see you in ten minutes! Sit there!' She pushed Ellen onto the steps and whipped off her cap. 'Take your hands away or you'll get your fingers cut. Now, undo your plait, or I'll cut it off as it is.'

Ellen did as Goldie ordered, cringing as she heard the first snip of the scissors.

Goldie dropped a small curl onto Ellen's lap. 'See! I'm only snipping a bit off! It has to be done, so you may as well get it over with; or you'll be getting me into trouble as well as yourself and I'm not having that!'

Ellen crouched dolefully on the edge of the step as Goldie snipped away at her hair. Every so often Goldie dropped a small curl in front of her and it was only when Doris said, 'Stop it, Goldie,' that she looked up in alarm.

Behind her on the ground lay large clumps of her hair! She leapt to her feet, clutching at her head. 'You've scalped me, you rotter!' She was ready to spring at Goldie, her fingers spread like claws, when a warning sound from Doris halted her.

Mrs Garland was at the kitchen door, coming to see what all the noise was about.

'Can't I leave you out of my sight for a minute, before you act like a pair of alley cats?' she demanded, striding forth, flailing her hands at their heads.

She suddenly stopped. 'Oh, lawdy me! Just look at the sight of you! Give them scissors to me, Goldie! Eeh, you'll go too far one of these days, milady!' She aimed a clout at Goldie but missed and turned her attention to Ellen. 'Get that cap back on your head, Ellen. You won't look so bad if it's covered up. And be thankful it'll grow again! Now, come in for something to eat. And no more shenanigans!' Muttering that she didn't know what the world was coming to, she stamped her way back inside.

'I'll get you back!' Ellen threatened Goldie. 'Just see if I don't!'

Goldie laughed carelessly. 'You'll be a fool if you try! You're a nobody in this household! And don't forget, I'm senior to you. You'll do as you're told ... and like it!'

Goldie's words spoke the stark truth. Day followed day; each one filled with a frenzy of activity of cleaning, scrubbing, dusting and washing. 'Clean the pans, Ellen. Fetch the coal, Ellen. Empty the slops, Ellen. Scour the chamber pots, Ellen.'

Goldie took great delight in giving her the more distasteful tasks, her narrowed eyes daring her to refuse. Well, she wasn't that stupid! And she'd done far worse things at home helping her mam with the little ones! But, by heck, here it took six of them to run around after a family of four! Not that she saw much of the son and daughter of the family ... or Mr Oldfield for that matter.

There was a girl, Miss Sarah, who looked as if she was about thirteen or fourteen – a right stuck-up little madam, who didn't pick a thing up from off her bedroom floor, according to Nora.

Master John, now, he were nice! Smiled at her, if he saw her on the corridor when she'd got on with her other jobs and was allowed to help Nora with a bit of upstairs cleaning. Twelve, he was, just over a year older than herself, and away at school in Manchester throughout the week but came home at the weekends. Caught him sliding down the banister, she had ... and wished she could join him! And he knew it!

'Go on. I won't tell,' he had offered.

But she had shaken her head and scurried back to the kitchen.

By the end of each day, she was fair

whacked. Her fingernails were broken from the daily rubbing of the black leading over kitchen-range bars and by the time she had backed her way from one end of the kitchen to the other, scrubbing at the red-tiled floor, her knees were as numb as ninepence and her shoulders ached fit to drop off.

The weeks and months sped by. She forgot what it was like to curl up with a book by the fireside or to play out with her friends when her homework and household chores had been completed to her mam's satis-faction. Here, her whole life was a chore.

Christmas passed by in a whirl of activity, but the staff received a gift on Boxing Day as they lined up in the hallway. A plain white handkerchief was Ellen's gift from Mrs Old-field and from Mr Oldfield a penny. Goldie received a handkerchief and a small square of soap and a threepenny bit, but Doris was given the same as Ellen.

January came and snow covered the hills and moors. The harsh winter lasted for weeks, bringing them not only the inconveni-ence of being snowed in, but also the unfet-tered joy of stolen moments of snowball fights and toboggan slides, when they were sometimes joined by Master John, whose mother was blissfully unaware of her son's plebeian activities.

February's rain was blown aside by the mad March winds and the air was fresh and clean. Daffodils danced in their thousands in the woodlands, the churchyard and the country lanes.

One day in April, a week after Easter, Ellen was sitting on a stool, a bucket of carrots at her feet, a box to catch the peelings on her knee and a sacking of coarse hessian tied around her middle. She was daydreaming of the wonderful time they had had at the Easter fair that had taken place on the lower slopes of Rivington Pike. Grandpa had given her two whole pennies to spend and she and Doris had had the time of their lives choosing which sweets to buy and gazing starry-eyed at the various stalls and sideshows. Eeh, they had nowt like that where she'd lived before!

She was suddenly aware that Master John had come down the steps to the lower level of the kitchen. He picked up a cherry bun that was cooling on a wire tray along with two dozen others and bit into it with appreciation.

'Now, Master John, what are you up to ... apart from eating my cakes, that is?' Cook wanted to know.

John brushed the crumbs from around his mouth with the back of his hand. 'Mama says Sarah and I may have a picnic down by the stream, if someone can be spared to accompany us. Do say yes, Cookie dear. You know how delicious everything tastes out of doors.'

Ellen looked up with interest. A picnic sounded a wonderful idea. Who would Cook spare to go with them? Her hands were suspended in mid-action, as she waited breathlessly for Cook's response.

'I know nothing of the sort, Master John, and don't think you can wheedle me into anything you ask, just because you come in here paying compliments.' The smile on her face belied her words and John knew his request was granted, even before he entwined his arms halfway around her ample middle. 'Get on with you, Master John. What weather is this for a picnic? You'll catch your deaths of cold, you will.'

'No, honestly, Cook, it really is quite warm. The sun is shining and we can't waste this beautiful day. You know I go back to school next week.'

'Well, as long as your mama says so, Master John. What would you like?'

John sniffed the air. 'Fresh-baked bread

rolls, for a start. And how about some of that lovely ham we had yesterday ... if there's any left, that is! And...' he cast his eye around the kitchen '...some of these cherry buns and a jar of your excellent strawberry jam, that we can spread ourselves.'

Mrs Garland smiled indulgently at him. 'Right-e-o! Off you go and tell Miss Sarah to get ready. Well see to everything down here.'

John whooped with joy and bounded up the steps in two leaps. Good old Cookie. He knew she'd agree.

'Good old Cookie' looked around at the kitchen girls, from Ellen's hopeful face to Goldie's disdainful one. Doris looked caught in the middle, half-hoping to be chosen but wary of displeasing Goldie. Cook knew who would enjoy it most ... but also understood the kitchen hierarchy. She wasn't born yesterday. 'Right, Goldie! You're the eldest. Go and get your old clothes on and get a bag out of the cupboard under the stairs to carry the picnic in.'

Ellen's face fell. She had hoped...! She sighed as she picked up another carrot and began to hack at its skin.

Goldie flashed Cook a defiant look, her knuckles on her hips. 'Why me? I don't want

41

to play nursemaid to a couple of kids. Let them carry their own picnic, if that's what they want. It'll be cold and wet by the stream and I'll be the one to freeze to death!'

Cook frowned. 'You can think yourself lucky that the missus isn't down here, hearing you talking like that. All right, what about you, Doris?'

Doris looked up eagerly. 'Oh, yes. I'd like ... that is I'm not sure ... I ... er...' Her voice tailed away under Goldie's withering scorn.

'Suit yourself!'

Ellen held her breath.

'It'll have to be you, Ellen.'

Ellen jumped up, scattering carrots across the floor. 'Oh, yes please, Cook! Golly! That'll be lovely. Oh, yes! Where's the bag you want?'

In great excitement, Ellen found a small wicker basket in a cupboard and jumped from foot to foot as Cook filled it with goodies for the picnic, adding two large bottles of her homemade lemonade.

Cook weighed the basket in her hands. 'On second thoughts, you'll never carry this by yourself, Ellen, and you're a bit young to be in charge of Master John and Miss Sarah.'

Ellen's heart sank. She could see Goldie's smirk and she glared at her. It wasn't fair, not after her getting it all ready.

'I think I'd best send Nora with you, since there's only Mrs Oldfield's lunch to see to ... and Goldie can serve that,' Cook decided. 'Go and get your old frock on. I can't have you ruining this one. And get your shawl. For all Master John says, there's a bit of a cold wind blowing.'

Cold wind or not, Ellen skipped along the road and down a grassy path to the nearby stream, holding one handle of the basket while Nora held the other. They made for a part of the stream where there was a rocky outcrop forming a small waterfall, making it an ideal place for scrambling over the rocks and audaciously leaping across the stream.

Once Nora had settled herself down in a sheltered spot, her legs wrapped up in the blanket that she had carried, she shooed the three youngsters away, to leave her in peace while she read a ladies' pamphlet that was making popular inroads amongst the fortunate young women in service who could read and write.

Ellen and Master John ran across the grassy bank to the rocks, whilst Miss Sarah fastidiously picked her way more carefully, lifting her skirt to save it trailing on the wet ground, already regretting her rash moment of sisterly generosity in promising her brother a treat before he returned to his school.

Whilst John and Ellen tried to catch some tiddlers in an old bucket John had brought for that very purpose, Miss Sarah gathered brightly coloured flowers that she could press and use to make a picture when she went home, and then got out her sketch pad. She knew she wasn't particularly talented at drawing but it was an easy occupation and, above all, it pleased her mama.

By the time pangs of hunger drove John and Ellen back to Nora's side, Miss Sarah was already seated prettily on a rock, with a feather cushion under her that Cook had thought to put in the basket. John flung himself down on the stony ground, scattering a spray of tiny pebbles and soil across the red-and-white checked cloth.

Miss Sarah drew back her skirt in alarm. 'Really, John! I'm amazed that Mama ever let you out of the nursery! Your manners are appalling!'

'Quite right, Miss Sarah!' Nora agreed, shooing him off the cloth. 'Sit there at the edge, Master John, and tuck in. Cook has packed lots of things for you. Come on, Ellen. You as well.'

Ellen felt so happy she thought she might

burst! She wished the day might never end ... but of course it did. Nora packed the few remains of the picnic into the basket, whilst Miss Sarah watched her, still perched upon her cushion.

John and Ellen had a last run about the bank of the stream, shouting and laughing. Ellen boldly pulled the back hem of her frock forwards through her legs and tucked the ends of it into her belt at the front, and did a series of cartwheels, much to John's admiration.

'Hey! You're not bad ... for a girl!'

The perfect day was marred for her, as she walked back with Nora, again sharing the weight of the basket between them. The words carried clearly in the afternoon air.

'But she's so common, John! Her accent is appalling! And doing cartwheels like that! Mama would have a fit if she knew!'

Nora looked down at her young colleague, hoping that she hadn't heard, but one glance at her flushed face revealed that she had.

The following Sunday afternoon was one of Ellen's twice-monthly half-days off. She sped along to her grandparents' house, her heart pounding as she thought of her 'great idea'.

'So you see, Grandma, I'm not going to be called "common" no more; not by Miss Sarah, nor by nob'dy else. I want to get on and maybe get to be a lady's maid one day, like Nora. Or even better than that. I was always top o't'class at school – but I've got to learn how to speak proper an' lots of other things. D'you know what I mean? Will you and Grandpa 'elp me?'

Dorcas nodded in approval. 'Indeed we will, Ellen. With a bit of determination, you can be whatever you want to be.'

Spring passed and summer arrived with its long hot days and, for John, the long holiday from school. With going to school in Manchester, he didn't know any local lads and his mama wouldn't allow him to mix with them anyway as they were 'too common'. And the local middle-class families with similar-aged sons looked upon him with the same disdain. Consequently, he spent most of his time at home with his books, avidly devouring anything to do with locomotives and the power of steam. That was what he wanted to do when he was grown up; not the manufacturing of bricks, like his father.

He glanced through his bedroom window and saw Ellen going up the garden path swinging an empty bucket. His spirit lightened. She'd be going to get some vegetables off Jenkins, their gardener-cum-handyman. Since the springtime picnic together, he often sought her out for a chat. He had to choose the times carefully as he knew his mama would bring a halt to such impropriety, but it did help to pass the time by, and she seemed interested in what he did at school. She could even remember the details the next time they chatted! There weren't any girls at his school but he reckoned Ellen could match any of his classmates. He had even started lending her some of his books, putting one in the cupboard under the stairs opposite the library when he was home at the weekend and exchanging it the following week. Sometimes, she wrote a note on a scrap of paper, saying which parts she had liked best or a comment on the action. She didn't realize it, but she helped him write a more diverse critique for his homework.

She was a good sport, too, and had taken it in good part when he had startled her with a good aim from his peashooter one morning when she was brushing the carpet in the hallway. He closed his book and picked up a paper dart he had made earlier with a page he'd torn out of an exercise book. He quickly scribbled 'I bet you can't find me' on it and hurried outside into the garden.

A few minutes later, peering through the foliage of the hedge, he could see Ellen struggling back down the path, the bucket now heavy with vegetables. Stifling a giggle, he zoomed the dart over the hedge. He heard a gasp of surprise and saw her dump the bucket onto the path as she bent down to pick up the paper dart. Before she had time to peer through the hedge and see him, he darted into the canopy of the nearby willow tree and waited.

It wasn't long before he could see her creeping furtively along his side of the hedge. She stopped and stared at the willow tree. Although he could see her, he knew she couldn't see him through the dangling tendrils of foliage. However, she darted across the grass and then slowly approached. He waited until she was just a few inches away and was reaching out a tentative hand to part the foliage – then he grabbed hold of her and pulled her inside.

'Aargh!'

He clamped a hand over her mouth to cut off her yell of surprise. 'Got you!' he chortled, releasing his hold.

'I knew you were here!'

He grinned widely. 'I still got you! You should have seen your face!'

'You scared me to death,' she admitted, now grinning back at him.

John turned around with his arms spread wide. 'Isn't it great? It gets thicker every year. It makes a good den, doesn't it?' He flopped down on the circular seat that surrounded the base of the tree, patting the space beside him. 'We can meet here and talk about books and things. You make some interesting comments.'

Ellen didn't sit down but she blushed at the praise. 'I like reading. Books take you into another world. Will you lend me some of your other books?'

'You mean like mathematics and science, and history and geography?'

'Yes. I used to like history and geography at school. We never did any science, though, unless you count nature study.'

John agreed and Ellen said she had better get back to the kitchen before she was missed. She ran back to her bucket of vegetables with a lighter heart. Life was getting better. Over the past few months, Nora had been lending her a small notebook containing helpful hints for ladies' maids – recipes for hair-washing, skin preparations and suchlike. Her grandma had given her a similar notebook and she copied Nora's notes into it whenever she had some free time, much to Goldie's amused scorn.

'Somebody'd have to be hard up to take you on as a lady's maid!' she taunted her. 'You can't make a silk purse out a pig's ear!'

As Goldie turned away, Ellen squashed up her nose and snorted like a pig. Doris laughed, making Goldie whirl around to see what was funny but both girls ignored her.

A few days later, Nora asked Ellen for her notebook.

'I left it there on the dresser for you,' Ellen told her. 'I thought you'd taken it.'

'I haven't seen it since I lent it to you this morning. I need it later to write down a new recipe for a skin lotion I've seen in a magazine.'

Nora left the kitchen and Ellen went over to the dresser, pulling open the drawers in case someone had put it inside. She looked at the various shelves and work-surfaces, wondering if she'd absent-mindedly left it somewhere else, but she couldn't find it.

Doris looked uncomfortable. She was seated on a stool with a small bowl of water on her lap, peeling potatoes. She looked down, as if concentrating on what she was doing.

'What's the matter?' Ellen asked sharply.

'Nothing!' Doris's face flushed and she wouldn't meet Ellen's gaze. She rinsed the potato in the bowl of water, dropped it into a bucket on her other side and then picked up another one, still avoiding eye contact.

'Well, something's up. What is it?'

'Nothing! That is...' She glanced at the bucket of vegetable peelings at her feet, but then shook her head. 'I daren't tell you. Goldie'd kill me!'

'Why? What's she done?'

As she spoke, Ellen suddenly grasped the meaning of Doris's agitated glances at the bucket of peelings. She darted over to it and plunged her hands into the wet peelings. A few inches down, her fingers felt the texture of paper and she pulled out Nora's book, looking in disbelief at the sodden pages of blotched writing.

'It's ruined!' she cried. 'Why didn't you stop her?'

Doris shrugged, biting her lower lip. 'I couldn't. You know what she's like.'

Ellen felt like crying. It wouldn't have been so bad if Goldie had ruined her book. She could have started over again. But to ruin Nora's! Just wait until she saw her!

Right on cue, Goldie clattered down the steps. She paused when she saw what Ellen was holding and then grinned. 'Had a careless accident? Nora won't be too pleased, will she?'

'You know it wasn't an accident, Goldie! You're right spiteful!' Ellen burst out. Why can't you mind your own business and keep out of mine?'

Goldie's eyes opened wide in innocent pretence. 'I don't know what you're talking about. And you needn't think you frighten me, glaring at me, like that!' She flicked the duster in her hand at Ellen's face as she flounced past.

Ellen grabbed at the end of the flicked duster and yanked it towards her. Goldie was caught off balance and staggered forwards. Ellen grabbed Doris's bowl of water and flung it towards Goldie, the cold water drenching her. Goldie yelled with rage and darted towards Ellen to retaliate in some fashion but slipped on the wet tiles and skidded across the kitchen floor on her backside, taking Ellen down with her ... just as Cook came in from the storeroom, carrying a trayload of flour, sugar, raisins and eggs.

Cook's cry of 'Lawdy me!' accompanied

the crash as her trayload slipped from her hands, its spilled contents adding to the mess and confusion. The two on the floor were yelling and screaming, pulling hair and slapping wherever their hands landed.

Cook picked up a wooden spoon and banged it against the base of a heavy pan ... the only way to get their attention. Their struggles ceased and they stared up at her, a guilty flush spreading across both faces.

'It was Ellen! She started it all!' Goldie burst out.

'No, it wasn't! It was you!'

'Stop this at once! I'll have none of this fighting in my kitchen! Do you hear?'

Cook's red face quelled further argument and they stood before her, trembling with both anger and the awareness of the possible consequences that might await them.

Cook was furious. 'You're behaving no better than them wild animals Lord Lever's put in his park! I'll speak to you both later when this meal has been got out of the way. Now, get this mess cleaned up at once! And not one word between the two of you! No, not you, Doris. Them as made the mess can clean it! And double quick, if you want to keep your jobs!'

Ellen was mortified. So much for trying to

act like a lady! Whatever had come over her? What if Cook got rid of them both? However would she be able to tell her grandma?

'What did Goldie have to say for herself?' Nora, who had missed it all while she was upstairs dressing Mrs Oldfield's hair, asked later.

'Well, you know Goldie! Said she'd never seen your book! Though it didn't get into that bucket by itself, did it! I've told her she's to buy you a new notebook and Ellen has to copy all your notes into it. That'll make 'em think twice before any more shenanigans like that.'

Nora nodded. 'Eeh, fancy Ellen standing up to her like that! You never know, though,' she said hopefully. 'It might have done Goldie some good.'

'Aye, you could be right. They're both good workers. I'd be sorry to lose either of them. Young Ellen will go far, the way she's learning. Give her another year or so and I reckon she'll be doing more than pushing Goldie's nose out of joint!'

Three

1904

'More coffee for Mr Oldfield, Harris,' Mrs Oldfield ordered, 'and a jug of hot water. And make sure it is very hot this time. My coffee is practically cold.'

'Certainly, ma'am. Would anyone like more toast?' Ellen asked, smiling around at the family, as they neared the completion of their breakfast. It was four years since she had come to work for the Oldfields and she was a 'tweeny' now, with duties both above and below stairs. No more scrubbing floors for her! Patty, their new kitchen maid, did that.

'Yes, please. Two more slices for me,' Mr John, who was home from his school for the weekend, accepted her offer. 'I must ask Mrs Garland if I may take a jar of her marmalade back to school with me. Will you tell her I will come down to the kitchen for it later, Harris?'

'Certainly, Mr John.'

'Really, John!' Mrs Oldfield said sharply. 'There is no need whatsoever for you to go down to the kitchen. Harris will tell Mrs Garland to put a jar into your tuck box.'

Ellen hid a smile. His mother didn't realize just how often her son did appear in the kitchen, or in the kitchen garden, or upstairs on the corridor when she was sweeping the carpet or doing some other household task. She felt sure his announcing an intended visit to the kitchen was a ploy to let her know he planned to make an opportunity to chat with her later in the day and she was looking forward to discussing the latest activities of the Women's Social and Political Union, that were hitting the headlines in the daily newspapers she read after Bert had finished with them. Although not altogether agreeing with their militant tactics, she was eager to hear John's views on the movement.

Mr Oldfield was opening a letter that Cadman had just given to him. 'Oh dear!' He glanced at his wife and then at their maid. 'I think you'd better sit down, Harris.'

'Indeed, she won't!' Mrs Oldfield snapped. 'What a suggestion! Get about your business, Harris! More coffee, wasn't it? And toast for Mr John.'

Ellen didn't move. Something was up ... and it concerned her.

'Sir?' she queried.

John looked concerned also. 'What is it, Father?'

Mr Oldfield reached out and touched her hand. It wasn't a thing he normally did and it increased Ellen's anxiety. 'It's a note from your grandmother, Harris, asking if you can be spared from work today.'

Mrs Oldfield's face turned purple. 'Spared from work? Indeed, she can't!'

'Hush, my dear.' He held up a hand towards his wife, stilling her indignant response. He turned back to face Ellen, a look of compassion in his eyes. 'I'm sorry to have to tell you, Harris ... but it appears that your grandfather died this morning.'

The next few days were difficult for Ellen. She felt as though she were physically carrying a heavy lead weight in her heart.

Mr Oldfield had taken her to her grandma's house on his way to the brickworks, much to his wife's disapproval. It was the first time she had travelled in a horse-drawn carriage but she was too distraught to enjoy the experience. John accompanied them and also made the return journey at the end of the afternoon to walk back with her, though she was certain his mother wasn't aware of his gallantry. He had actually put his arm around her in a gesture of condolence and Ellen had found his concern for her a comfort.

Ellen was given two hours off work to attend her grandfather's funeral, on the understanding that she would make up the hours from her next allocated half-day off. No one came from Manchester. Her mam couldn't take a day off work and it was so long since Grandpa and Grandma had left the area that they seemed like distant relatives – except to Ellen. She was the one who would miss Grandpa most; after Grandma, that was.

The next time she visited her grandma, Abram's absence was tangible. Ellen missed him greatly. His gentle kindness had soon dispelled her distrust of him and had gone some way to ease her distrust of men in general ... and he had always encouraged her self-esteem.

Dorcas, too, had mellowed much over the past four years and was truly fond of her granddaughter. 'You're a good girl, Ellen,' she told her, patting her hand. 'It was the best thing we ever did, bringing you here. You're making something good of your life and you're a great comfort to me.'

Over the next few weeks, Ellen sensed her grandma was troubled about something. 'Is it the house, Grandma? Do you have to find somewhere else to live?' She knew many workers' houses were tied to the job.

Dorcas shook her head. 'Not immediately. The rent is paid until the end of the quarter. No, it's your Auntie Bessie. That husband of hers has got her pregnant again ... and she's forty-two. She's not strong enough.'

'My cousin Lizzie will be able to help, won't she?'

'Aye, she'll have to ... and that's another thing. She's only a few years older than you but what sort of life has she got? She already does most of the looking after of the younger children. It's time someone thought about Lizzie.'

Six weeks later, the sad news that Bessie had died in childbirth was sent by Lizzie to her grandma. Ellen was shocked when she heard and more so when her grandma told her she intended to return to Manchester to look after Bessie's children.

'Oh, Grandma, no! What will I do without you?'

Dorcas clasped both of Ellen's hands in

hers. 'I know this won't be easy for you, Ellen, but I'm doing it for Lizzie. She's nothing better than a skivvy for her dad and the children. She has a young man but it's impossible for her to think of marrying him. Their house is overcrowded as it is.' Dorcas paused, weighing her words carefully. 'Abram and I had a sum of money put by for when he reached retirement age, so I am intending to use it to buy a house where I can live with Lizzie and the little ones. If Alf wants to stay with his children, then he can come too, but on my terms.'

Ellen looked at her in dismay. Maybe she should return also? But she dreaded moving back anywhere near to Zach Durban! She pushed her anxious thoughts away and thought of Lizzie instead. 'You're right, Grandma. I'm being selfish. It's time Lizzie had some help. It's a wonderful idea ... but I shall miss you dreadfully.'

The seasons flew by. Two more summers and autumns; two winters and springs. The new Labour Party was formed, free meals were given to needy families. There was even talk that plans were afoot to allow elderly people to retire from work with a small allocation of money to support them. A pension, it was to

60

be called.

'I doubt it will come in my day,' Mrs Garland declared pessimistically. 'You don't get owt for nowt in my experience. We working folk'll always have to work hard for our living.'

It was late in May. The annual spring-cleaning was almost completed and everyone needed a rest. Not that that the servants would get one.

Nora was particularly disgruntled as she and Ellen knelt side by side, a stiff hand-brush in their hands as they backed their way along the carpet on the first floor landing, meticulously brushing the carpet.

'You should have seen the state of Miss Sarah's room. Clothes dropped all over the place and her cupboard drawers all higgledy-piggledy,' she grumbled. 'She's right untidy.'

Ellen made a sympathetic sound. She never went inside the bedrooms. They were Nora's domain. 'You're a grump this morning, Nora. What's the matter?'

'Oh, I'm just a bit fed up. I was talking to Mrs Dearden's maid on my afternoon off yesterday. She gets more money than I do and gets an extra full day off every month. Mrs Dearden belongs to the Suffragists' Society and treats her servants like human beings. It's a bit like slave labour here, by comparison.'

'More work and less talk would give you more time to get your work done!' Mrs Oldfield's sharp tones snapped from behind them.

Nora and Ellen exchanged a quick, guilty glance, wondering how much she had overheard. Keeping their heads down, they hastily shuffled aside to allow Mrs Oldfield to pass between them and continue on her way to the top of the stairs. They didn't dare to speak until their employer had reached the ground floor and they heard the living room door close.

'Oh, heck!' Nora muttered. 'She'll have it in for me for the rest of the day, now.'

It was Tuesday, Ellen's twice-monthly afternoon off, since her grandma wasn't there to visit on Sundays. As soon as lunch was over, she slipped into town, glad to be out of the house and enjoying the warm sunshine. She loitered along Lee Lane, admiring the display of cakes in Waddicor's cake shop before crossing over the road and going into Prince's Arcade to see what that week's show was at the Prince's Theatre. Not that she would ever get to see a show there. Her few hours off ended at half past four and she had just heard a quarter to four strike on the church clock.

She eyed the bicycles outside Frank Hart's bicycle shop. She wouldn't mind trying one of those one day, if she could ever save up enough to afford one, that was. It would get her into town a lot quicker than walking.

But, enough daydreaming. She needed to be heading back. She stopped at Trickett's toffee shop to buy half a penny's worth of pear drops. They were her favourites, half lemon and half raspberry, mmm! She popped one into her mouth, sucking its sweet taste as she hurried back up Church Street and down Chapel Lane, hoping she wasn't late.

As soon as she entered the kitchen she could tell that something was wrong. Patty and Doris were openly crying and Goldie was looking decidedly upset. Even Cook and Bert seemed barely in control of their emotions.

'What's the matter?' She looked around the kitchen. 'And where's Nora?'

'She's gone.' Cook's voice sounded bleak.

Doris immediately began to wail and Patty huddled to her side.

'Gone? What d'you mean? Where has she gone?'

'Sacked. Told to go. Just like that.'

'Sacked? But, why?' Ellen was totally bewildered. 'I don't understand.'

'A ring's gone missing. Miss Sarah's diamond star.'

'It's probably just lost somewhere. Nora was only saying this morning how untidy Miss Sarah is. But why do they think Nora's taken it? She wouldn't dream of stealing!'

'Apparently, Mrs Oldfield heard her grumbling about her pay this morning and put two and two together – and made half a dozen!' Cook looked around at them all. 'I ask you! What sort of evidence is that? Did you hear her grumbling, Ellen?'

Ellen felt her cheeks flame. 'Well, yes, she did, but it doesn't mean she's stolen Miss Sarah's ring, does it?' She took her shawl off and fastened on her apron. 'I've a good mind to go and tell Mrs Oldfield what I think of her! She can't do this! It's not fair!'

Mrs Garland put out a hand to restrain her. 'It's no use, Ellen. I did what I could and so did Bert. Mrs Oldfield said if there was one more word, we'd all get the sack – and that wouldn't help anyone, let alone Nora.' She sighed heavily and pulled herself to her feet, looking as though she had lost all heart to continue. 'Come on, girls. We've got to get dinner served. Ellen, you'll have to help Bert and Goldie in the dining room. We'll do the best we can down here.'

The next few days were the worst any of them could remember. Everyone did their work with long faces, a contrast to the usual busy hum of chatter that filled the kitchen. On his next day off, Bert made tentative inquiries about Nora to try to find out where she might have gone – but no one knew anything. She had left the area without leaving a trace.

Cook redeployed her staff. 'Ellen, you'd better see to Miss Sarah. Goldie can see to Mrs Oldfield. Doris and Patty, you'll have to work extra hard down here. We should be able to manage for a couple of days but we'll have to get up sharp in the morning; and you'll all have to say goodbye to your afternoons off till we get someone to take Nora's place.'

Nora's job was advertised and the servants waited anxiously to see who would be appointed. Two applicants got no further than being shown round the upstairs rooms, with Mrs Oldfield's stringent demands ringing in their ears. Another applicant started but only stayed a week, saying too much was demanded of her for such a meagre wage. Another was sacked after two days for being lazy and insolent.

Mrs Oldfield was standing over them, checking and rechecking what they were doing and constantly reprimanding them for taking too long over their tasks, no account being made of the extra work being demanded of them. Eventually, Mrs Garland asked permission to speak with Mrs Oldfield. She had an idea how they might resolve the problem.

Mrs Oldfield received her in the parlour, whilst she was sipping her mid-morning cup of excellent coffee. 'I hope everything is under control in the kitchen, Mrs Garland. You know that Mrs Ingham is coming to lunch.'

Mrs Garland bobbed a slight curtsey. 'Yes, ma'am. All preparations are under way. The thing is, ma'am, I've been having a think over who's to take Nora's, that is, Tucker's, place, and, what with all the disappointments we've had with them who's tried, I'm hoping you won't mind me taking the liberty of coming up with a suggestion.' She paused, wondering nervously if she was overstepping her position.

'Do get on with it, Mrs Garland. You're always telling me how difficult it is downstairs now that you are a hand down.'

'Yes, ma'am. That's what I want to speak with you about,' continued Mrs Garland, thankful that the opening had been made. 'It seems to me, ma'am, that we've been going about it the wrong way.'

Mrs Oldfield straightened her posture, her expression chilled. 'Are you suggesting, Mrs Garland, that I am not competent enough to set about employing my own staff?'

'Oh, no, ma'am! Not you! Er, my advice is what I mean. I've, er, been having a rethink and come to the conclusion that it's not a new lady's maid we need, not when we have two very satisfactory "tweeny" maids already in employment. What we need, ma'am, begging your pardon, is another kitchen maid. Somebody to start at the bottom and give Goldie ... I mean Goulding and Harris a chance to prove themselves as lady's maids.'

Fay Oldfield regarded the woman in front of her. She suspected she was being manipulated – and she didn't like it. However, she was shrewd enough to realize that what Mrs Garland was saying made sense – and it would cost less to promote the two 'tweenies' than to employ a lady's maid. Furthermore, this way, she got two lady's maids for less than the price of one.

The heavy silence became too much for Mrs Garland. She bobbed another curtsey. 'I'd best be getting back to the kitchen, ma'am.'

'Wait, Mrs Garland; you could be right. Miss Sarah is growing up and could do with a personal maid of her own, especially as she is now out in society.' Mrs Oldfield's posture relaxed a little and she sipped her coffee again. 'Yes. I will give your suggestion some thought and I will let you know my decision forthwith. Thank you, Mrs Garland.'

Thus dismissed, Mrs Garland thankfully made her way back to the kitchen. At least she hadn't been thrown out on her ear and, maybe, Mrs Oldfield might give serious thought to her idea. Time would tell.

Two days later, Goldie and Ellen were summoned to the parlour. They listened in awed silence to what Mrs Oldfield was saying to them.

'This, of course, is a temporary arrangement, until I am satisfied that you can do the work satisfactorily.'

Both girls nodded, murmuring, 'Yes, ma'am,' as they bobbed a brief curtsey.

'You, Goulding, will take the senior position of being my maid.'

'Yes, ma'am.'

'And you, Harris, under my close supervision, will be Miss Sarah's maid. I am sure Goulding will give you helpful advice on what to do.'

Goldie grinned triumphantly at Ellen as she murmured, 'Yes, ma'am,' still hardly daring to believe what they had been told. It was the chance she had been waiting for. It was a pity the way it had come about but she knew that Nora would have been pleased that it was them, rather than anybody else. They hurried back to the kitchen with their exciting news.

Mrs Garland beamed her pleasure at them. 'Now, don't be putting on airs and graces, the pair of you. I'll still need you down here at times, especially until we get another kitchen maid to help Doris and Patty. And, I tell you what, Doris. You can be the chief kitchen maid, for the time being. I'll give you an extra penny a week and see how you get on.'

Doris joined in the beaming faces. It was the best time they had had since Nora left.

Four

1907

'Really, Harris, I declare this pattern must be at fault!'

Miss Sarah's peevish tones cut through the oppressive afternoon air. It was August. Most of Horwich's 'society' had removed themselves to more picturesque areas of the county. Some had even ventured down south or abroad. Wherever they had gone, Miss Sarah was pining for select company; anyone who would relieve her from this dreadful monotony!

Ellen's fine-pointed needle hovered over the piece of lace that she was attaching to Miss Sarah's new evening gown. She put down the lace and glanced over to where Miss Sarah was furiously plucking at the offending stitches. 'Shall I see to it, Miss Sarah?' she offered, well used to her young mistress's impatience with the intricacies of needlework.

Miss Sarah tossed the article onto the

plush seat beside her. 'I'm bored, Harris! Bored! I've seen no one ... no one, I tell you, for absolutely ages! It's all very well Mama saying that Papa can't leave the business at the moment but everyone else has left town and we are left here on our own. It's so humiliating!'

'Miss Bartlett called on Monday last,' Ellen reminded her, 'and Miss Knighton and her sister left cards on Tuesday whilst we were shopping in Bolton.'

'When I say "no one", Harris, you know perfectly well that I mean people of some importance. The Misses Bartlett and Knighton, whilst being acquaintances, are not ... you know, quite...' Miss Sarah left the sentence unfinished.

Yes, Ellen did know. There were only two classes, in the opinion of the two Oldfield ladies; those who were important and those who weren't. Plus, of course, the serving classes who were of no account whatsoever.

With a sudden sparkle, Miss Sarah whirled about to face Ellen. 'I know, Harris! Let us take some carriage exercise! I know Mama will agree. Put my gowns out on the bed and then go tell Cadman to send Jenkins's lad to order a carriage from Livesey's immediately. We will do a few turns about town. You never know whom we might see.' With a burst of enthusiasm, she whirled out of the room to seek out her mama.

Ellen carefully folded the gown she was altering and then draped various suitable afternoon gowns across the silk counterpane.

Leaving the gowns, she ran lightly down the stairs to pass the order on to Bert Cadman and then hurried back upstairs to her attic bedroom to change into a cast-off gown of Miss Sarah's that she had altered to fit her. It was of pale grey crêpe de Chine, fitting close to her hips and caught in a wide belt. She was thankful her grandma had passed on her sewing skills before she returned to Manchester.

She swiftly changed the ribbon and bow around the crown of her trusty straw hat and then hurried back to Miss Sarah's room, knowing that, left to herself, Miss Sarah would have all the gowns on the floor and with none of them deemed suitable.

Indeed, Miss Sarah was holding her fourth choice of garment in front of her, judging by the three gowns already strewn upon the floor. Ellen swept her glance over the ones already discarded, murmured a few 'hmms' and 'aahs' at the one Miss Sarah was holding against herself, and decisively picked up a lilac creation from amongst the ones still on the bed. A long-handled parasol, matching in colour and trim, added further elegance to the outfit and a wide-brimmed hat with a large, rounded crown, adorned with lilac-coloured silk roses, completed the look.

Having coaxed Miss Sarah into it, Ellen persuaded her to take a few turns in front of the mirror and they both declared the outfit to be 'just the thing' for this warm summer's day.

Being Miss Sarah's maid for over a year had increased Ellen's confidence and, when they were alone together, their conversation was almost that of friends – as long as Ellen re-membered to always show deference, of course.

Mr John was now at university in Cam-bridge. He was just as friendly towards her when he came home and gave her permission to borrow any of the books from his book-shelf whilst he was away. Miss Sarah also loaned her ladies' fashion magazines, thus in-advertently broadening her outlook further.

A discreet knock on the bedroom door announced the arrival of the hired carriage. The two girls hurried down the main stair-case and down the front steps to the await-ing vehicle. Cadman handed Miss Sarah up the step and then stood aside to allow Ellen to clamber up herself. He tipped her a wink as the carriage jerked on its way.

It was a pleasant ride into town and as they approached the main shopping area Miss Sarah instructed Ellen to tell the driver to drive more slowly. Even so, it didn't take them long to travel the whole length of Lee Lane as far as the Crown Hotel. This was where Chorley Old Road and Chorley New Road met and where the trams ended their journey from Bolton and were prepared for the return trip.

'I knew that no one would be here,' Miss Sarah sighed, 'and it is so hot, I am sure I am about to faint with the heat.'

'There's a shop that sells lovely ice cream just round the corner, Miss Sarah,' Ellen suggested. 'Why don't we buy a dish and eat it here in the carriage.'

'Hmm, I'm not sure it is quite the thing,' Miss Sarah objected, wrinkling her nose.

'But it would be fun,' Ellen coaxed, 'and, as you say, there is no one here to notice.'

'Very well, then. But I insist on stepping inside to make sure everywhere is clean before we buy. You never know what germs and other unmentionable things the lower classes leave behind.'

Ellen swivelled on her seat, uncomfortably aware that the driver had heard Miss Sarah's thoughtless comments. 'Stop outside Ferretti's Ice Cream Parlour, driver,' she instructed.

It was delightfully cool inside the shop. The cleanliness of the place was in no doubt and Miss Sarah was easily persuaded to cast her eye over the different authentic Italian ice creams the Ferretti family had introduced to Horwich. She had just completed her selection when Ellen's gaze was drawn outside. One of the new motor cars, driven by an elegantly dressed young man, was being edged past their carriage. But for the fact that a tram was passing from the other direction, there would have been plenty of room for the motor car – but the tram narrowed the space considerably and rumbled unfalteringly on its way.

The driver of the motor car tooted his horn impatiently, causing the horse to skitter nervously. Their carriage driver flicked his driving whip gently and the carriage moved forward a few yards. However, the young man scowled and stood up, remonstrating further. Angry words drifted in through the open window.

'Oh, dear! Whatever is happening out

there?' Miss Sarah murmured, moving closer to the window, in time to see the horse perform a skittish dance, taking the carriage backwards until it met the obstacle of the car's front fender.

As the young man leapt out of his motor car, his eyes were drawn to the two faces in the ice cream parlour window. More in a gesture of defiance than an act of gallantry, he raised his felt homburg and bowed stiffly from the waist before remonstrating further with their hired driver. After a further exchange of heated words, he returned to his vehicle and accelerated away with a defiant blast of his horn, followed by a derisory salute with his hand.

The carriage driver, shouting a stream of oaths at the fast-disappearing motor car, struggled to control his horse's skittish behaviour.

Miss Sarah blushed, as his words invaded the quiet air of the ice cream parlour through the open windows. 'Really!' she exclaimed. 'It's a pity we need to hire such a common man. Mama is forever asking Papa to purchase our own carriage.'

Ellen felt compelled to rise to their driver's defence. 'The young man was more at fault,' she argued. 'His manner was very over–'

76

Miss Sarah gave her a haughty stare. 'Harris, you must allow me to have the finer judgement here. The young man was obviously of upper-class background. I shall go and reprimand our driver this very minute. He ought to be more gracious to those who are his betters! Here, pay the account!' She delved into her reticule, thrust a sixpence into Ellen's hand and swept majestically out of the shop.

When Ellen emerged onto the pavement a few minutes later she was just in time to hear their driver say, 'As you please, miss.' He flicked his whip above the horse's back, clicked his tongue and proceeded down the road at a fast trot.

'What an insolent man!' Miss Sarah exclaimed, her face very red indeed. 'How dare he speak to me like that? I shall complain to his employer.'

Ellen glanced up and down the street. 'More to the point, Miss Sarah, how are we going to get home when we have eaten our ice cream?' She sighed, knowing the only solution wouldn't please Miss Sarah. We will have to take the tram as far as Ainsworth Avenue and walk from there. It isn't far.'

Miss Sarah looked at her aghast. 'Go on a tram? Indeed not! Mama would be incensed. Common people ride in trams! Just think what it might do to my carriage gown. No! I shall go back into the ice cream parlour, while you find some suitable means of returning me home.' She swept back into shop, leaving Ellen standing nonplussed on the pavement.

The street was almost deserted and the few people in view didn't look as if they would be able to help them out of their predicament. She knew Mr Ferretti owned a small horse-drawn cart that was driven around the streets, selling their delicious ice cream, but the thought of Miss Sarah being taken home in that caused a bubble of laughter to well up inside her.

No. Her only option was to make her way to Livesey's garage at Gorton Fold, along Lee Lane, make apologies for her mistress's hasty words, and hope there was a different driver to return her to Ferretti's so that Miss Sarah could be taken home again. The tram that had impeded the motor car's progress had made its turn at the terminus and was rumbling back towards her. She signalled to the driver to stop and climbed aboard.

It was only a few tram stops to where she had to get off at the Black Dog Hotel and walk up Winter Hey Lane but the tram had halved her journey. Phew, it was so hot ... and she hadn't even had a taste of the ice cream! Really, she wished Miss Sarah would give thought to the consequences of her sharp temper before she spoke. It was all very well being Miss 'High and Mighty' when she was in her own home but to dispense with their transport in such a summary fashion was high-handed to say the least!

Lost in her indignant thoughts, she was more than halfway up Winter Hey Lane when she noticed a motor car parked a few yards ahead. 'Ha!' Her hands rested on her hips for a fleeting moment while she took stock of the situation. Unless she was very much mistaken, it was the much-offending motor car with its driver, also standing hands on hips, regarding the front fender of his beloved possession.

She marched towards him, her heels making sharp tapping noises on the paving flags. 'You might well look at the damage you caused!' she declared abruptly, without preamble. 'I have never seen such disgraceful behaviour in all my life! Who do you think you are, frightening a poor horse like that?'

The man lifted his gaze, his initial bewildered expression changing into a sardonic smile as he realized the cause of her fury.

'My, my! What indignation!' He reached out and cupped her chin. 'Lost for words now, are you? May I say how ravishing your anger makes you, my dear?'

Ellen jerked her chin out of his hand and leaped backwards, her face flushed. 'How dare you! I'm not your "dear". And you aren't safe to be out on the roads in that ... that...' Her fury robbed her of her words and she had to resort to pointing to his gleaming machine.

'Ah! My motor car. Like it, do you? She's a real beauty, isn't she?' He slowly eyed her up and down. 'I wonder if you would respond to my touch as well as she does?' He took a step forward.

Ellen backed away. 'Don't you dare touch me again!'

She missed her footing and fell backwards, sitting down with an undignified bump. With more than her dignity hurt, she scrambled hastily to her feet, brushing aside his outstretched hand. She winced as her ankle took her weight. That hurt.

'You are a fiery miss, aren't you?' His glance was part admiration, part exasperation. 'And do stop panicking. What do you imagine I could do to you in the middle of a street in broad daylight?'

His eyes roamed over her and Ellen felt her cheeks getting hot. She tried to take a step away but her left foot gave her such a stab of intense pain that she bit hard on her lower lip. Not wanting to be beholden to this man for any act of chivalry, she tossed her head high. 'Good day, sir!' She swung away but almost crumpled to the ground as another shaft of pain seared her foot. 'Ouch!'

The young man gripped her elbow and Ellen felt panic rising within. She tried to pull away and man eventually released his grip.

'Do stop acting as though I am about to ravish you,' he snapped. 'I'll take you home and deliver you safely to your mama. Where do you live?'

His tone angered her but his words reduced her anxiety. 'I'm out with my mistress,' she said in a small voice. And then added more forcefully, 'It was our carriage you found to be so uncivilly blocking your way!'

He laughed. 'Ha! Still high-spirited, what!'

Her glare of defiance seemed to amuse him. 'Well? You have found me and repri-manded me! Now what are you going to do? You can either hobble your way back to your mistress or you can get into my motor car and I will reunite you with her myself.

Which is it to be?'

Ellen knew that she had no choice. She summoned the hauteur that she had learned from both Oldfield ladies. 'You may take me to Livesey's so that I may rehire our carriage.'

'Ho-ho! The uncouth fellow abandoned you, did he? Did you reprimand him also? I don't suppose your mistress was best pleased by that.'

He was grinning at her discomfort, though whether in approval of her mistress's supposed displeasure or in admiration of her audacity, Ellen wasn't sure.

'My mistress dismissed him.'

'Did she, indeed? Another firebrand, eh?' He laughed. 'And now she is faced with either the humiliation of requesting his return or walking home?'

He fingered his chin, as he considered their dilemma and his options. Unless he was very much mistaken, the other face at the window of the ice cream parlour was that of a fashionably dressed, upper-class young lady. An introduction might not go amiss, especially if he were in the role of 'knight errant'.

'Then you must allow me to return you to your mistress and redress the consequences of the unfortunate incident by conveying you both to her home.'

He opened the passenger door and tilted his head to one side, one eyebrow raised in query, awaiting her response.

Ellen hadn't missed his expression as he considered the situation; nor the sardonic curl of his lip when he regarded her. She didn't want to get into his motor car. Besides, Mrs Oldfield would be scandalized if she accepted this young man's offer. But what choice did she have? However, the mocking gleam in his eyes made her suspect that, if she were to refuse his offer, he would return to the scene and make the same offer to Miss Sarah in her absence.

She tentatively put her weight on her left foot. It had eased a little but she knew she wouldn't be able to walk as far as Livesey's, nor back down Winter Hey Lane to take a tram back to Ferretti's. Her only option was to leave the ultimate decision to Miss Sarah, whose sensibility towards social etiquette had been finely tuned by her mama.

Consequently, she drew herself tall and said with as much dignity as she could summon, 'Thank you, sir. I will accept your kind offer.'

He gave a mocking bow. 'Then allow me!'

Before she realized his intention, he swept

her up in his arms and deposited her somewhat unceremoniously onto the passenger
seat of the motor car. Her mortification was
swiftly replaced by a surge of fear. What if he
just drove off with her? Should she get out
whilst she had the chance? Where was the
door handle?

The man was busy doing something at the
front of the vehicle, turning some sort of
handle, it seemed. She must go now!

Too late! The engine burst into life; the
man hurried to the door on the driver's side
and leapt nimbly into the seat beside her.
She shrank away from him as he leaned
towards her.

'Don't you...!'

'You're a skittish little filly, aren't you?' he
drawled, as he reached across her to check
that her door was closed properly. His left
hand rested on her thigh. She stiffened.
Even through the thickness of her gown, she
could feel the suggestive squeeze.

Or was it her imagination? She glanced
sideways at him. He wasn't even looking at
her; he was putting on the eye-coverings she
had seen the young motorists wearing. He
then took hold of a lever that he manipulated into a different position and the motor
car lurched forward. He thrust the lever into

another position and their speed increased. Ellen couldn't help gripping the top edge of the door as they proceeded to the top of Winter Hey Lane and turned left onto Lee Lane, heading towards the Crown.

She forced herself to relax and settle against her seat, determined now to enjoy the experience. It was quite exciting, really. And people turned to stare as they passed by. Just wait till she told the others! Goldie would be green with envy.

Miss Sarah was delighted to be offered a lift home in the sparkling new motor car. She made a brief show of modest refusal but had no intention to persist.

The young man bowed most charmingly. 'Leslie Fairchild, at your service, ma'am. I can assure you that I am of a most respectable family.' He paused, noticing the look of shrewd interest pass over her face. 'And may I know whom I have the pleasure of escorting home?' He smiled endearingly into her eyes, before she lowered her eyelids, blushing in the most appropriate manner.

'Miss Sarah Oldfield. My father owns the brickworks at Brazley.'

His eyebrows rose fractionally. 'Ah, yes. I thought I recognized your lovely face. I have seen you at various social functions with your parents and hoped there might be the opportunity to make your acquaintance.' He bowed in exaggerated fashion 'Miss Sarah Oldfield, your carriage awaits you.'

Over the next few months, Leslie Fairchild became a frequent visitor to the Oldfields' home. Whether for luncheon, afternoon tea or dinner, the message would come, 'Set an extra place for Mr Fairchild, Mrs Garland.' And the servants would scurry to oblige, pleased that Miss Sarah had a young man who so obviously adored her.

Ellen was less enthralled and, while Goldie, Doris and a newly taken-on 'tweeny' called Agnes, exchanged tales of his charm, she remained uneasy ... and, for the first time in years, the old nightmare recurred, leaving her shaken.

As Miss Sarah's maid, she was obliged to act as chaperone to her young mistress if Mrs Oldfield had no wish to perform that role herself. At tea parties, family dinners, dances and picnics, she would retire to the background, to be on call only if required. If such occasions were indoors at the Oldfields' home, she sat quietly to one side, sewing or mending, trying to be 'invisible' – though the glances Leslie Fairchild sometimes cast her way made Ellen feel decidedly uncomfortable.

Miss Sarah didn't notice. She was falling in love.

Goldie suddenly became eager to work extra hours when it meant being able to wait on a table or twitch a feather duster around the plethora of ornaments and plant stands in the drawing room or parlour. Her fluttering eyes and coy gestures very quickly caught Mr Fairchild's eye. Here was a pretty maid who wasn't repelled by his advances!

They immediately had the measure of the other. The preliminary moves were played; the secret touch of a finger along the inner wrist; the carefully timed flutter of eyelashes; the squeeze of a pert buttock, delightfully placed within easy reach. Goldie knew how to thrust forward her firm young breasts as she 'innocently' collided with him in the hallway. A hasty glance up and down the hall and they were in the library, always deserted at this time of day. All pretence of 'play' vanished. Both had a need the other could satisfy. Her breasts delivered their promise, inflaming his desire. Her body arched into his, her firm belly moving sensuously against him. The rest was over in minutes, as he took her, there and then against the bookshelves, both of them panting in ecstatic bliss.

Leslie cupped her chin in his still-sweating palm. 'My! You're a little beauty, aren't you, my dear? I think we're going to have fun, you and I.' He fumbled in his pocket and withdrew a sixpence. 'I'm sure you can find something pretty to buy with this.' He patted his pocket. 'And there's plenty more where that came from.'

Goldie slipped it into her pocket. She gave a smile of satisfaction. It seemed she had landed herself a little gold mine. She drew his head down, her lips parted, ready to accept his searching tongue. A wild excitement surged deep within her. She could sense that his desire was rising again. She drew away, running her fingers over his wet lips.

'And there's plenty more where that came from, too.'

Five

Easter 1908

The whole house was in a buzz of excitement. The Oldfield family had been invited to spend the Easter weekend in a hotel in Buxton with Mr and Mrs Fairchild, the parents of Miss Sarah's 'gentleman friend', leaving all the household staff at home.

'So, unless we want to spend all the time the Oldfields are away cleaning non-stop,' Mrs Garland declared, 'we'd best get on with it. So get some elbow behind that polishing, Patty, or you'll not be going up the Pike with the others on Good Friday!'

That dire warning made Patty rub her duster with extra vigour. She didn't want to miss that! Neither did any of the others and they were tackling the annual spring-cleaning with unaccustomed enthusiasm.

'You could have knocked me down with a feather when Mrs Oldfield said the Fairchilds' maids were being taken instead of ours,' Mrs Garland had confided to Bert. 'I only hope as Goldie and Ellen don't feel their noses pushed out of joint.'

'Not them,' Bert accurately predicted. 'Not with the chance of some extra time off if they pull their socks up and get all of the cleaning done beforehand.'

On the Tuesday of the week before the holiday, Ellen accompanied Miss Sarah to a milliner's shop on Lee Lane, from where she was collecting a new hat for the motoring journey. After a lengthy discussion the previous week, the design had been agreed and the colour chosen. A large chiffon scarf was to be fitted over it, to secure it against the effects of the wind that such journeys incurred.

'I will be in here for an hour, Harris,' Miss Sarah announced, when they had been shown through to the private fitting room. 'Once you have divested me of my mantle, you may go to the haberdashery to collect the ivory lace and ribbon that we ordered last week. Be sure to come straight back, as I may need your assistance.'

Ellen took leave of her mistress and made her way to the haberdashery in Winter Hey Lane. It was a bright spring day. Just the sort of day that made a girl wish she could dance and sing as she tripped merrily along the paved streets.

As she was about to cross the street to the haberdashery she noticed a horse-drawn vehicle was approaching from the right. She patiently waited for it to pass but, instead, it slowed down and halted in front of her. The laughing eyes of its young driver made her heart leap a double somersault.

It was the young man who often delivered the milk, eggs, butter and cream to the large houses in town and, in particular, to the side door of their kitchen – an occurrence that had happened more and more often during the past few weeks. She had learned from other delivery boys that his name was Charlie Metcalfe, the youngest son of the farmer who supplied their dairy produce.

Sometimes, he winked at her, as he did now, making her blush furiously. She knew he admired her and they had exchanged some light-hearted banter. Now, the sight of his laughing brown eyes set her heart racing.

Charlie raised his cap, smiling broadly. 'Afternoon, miss. Can I offer you a lift home?' His glance indicated the empty space beside him on the wooden seat of the dairy cart.

Ellen was thankful that she was dressed in a becoming outfit, another cast-off of Miss Sarah's. It was dark green and complemented her shining mass of curls, upon which her hat was sitting at a jaunty angle. The depth of his chocolate brown eyes – eyes that were regarding her in obvious admiration – made her heart do a double somersault. Time seemed to stand still. Was she grinning idiotically at him? She pulled herself together.

'I'm sorry. I can't. I'm with Miss Sarah ... Miss Oldfield, that is. We're out shopping,' she added needlessly. Her voice sounded strange to her ears and her heart was thumping so loudly he surely must hear it!

A klaxon horn sounded imperiously from one of the new motor cars that were becoming almost commonplace in every town. Its sound penetrated the aura around them and the young man glanced at it over her shoulder. 'I'll take you for a ride in one of those one day,' he promised, as he began to gather the reins in his strong hands.

Ellen's joy faltered as the car passed by on the other side of the road. She didn't tell him she had already ridden in that very one. Thankful that she had had her back towards Mr Fairchild, she said pertly, 'I haven't said I'd want to.'

He laughed. 'No, you haven't ... but you will.'

Ellen turned and began to walk a little way back up the street, assuming a haughty expression. She'd seen enough from Miss Sarah to be able to imitate that!

Charlie clicked the horse into a steady motion, matching her progress. 'I hear the Oldfields are going away next week,' he commented.

'Really? They have told you their plans, have they?'

'Aye!' At her look of disbelief, he added with a grin, They've cancelled part of the milk order. From the amount we've to deliver, I worked out they were leaving some of you behind. Are you one of them?'

'And why should I tell you that?' she countered, her heart beating quickly.

'I just thought you might like come up the Pike with me on Good Friday ... and maybe come out some of the other days while they're all away. What d'you say?'

Ellen's heart felt as if it were about to stop beating. 'I might. What time did you have in mind?'

'As soon as my milk round is over. Shall I call at the house for you?'

Ellen thought quickly. 'No, better not. We're not supposed to have "callers". I'll go as planned with the other girls and ... er ...

see you somewhere up there.' It was better that way. Then if he changed his mind, no one would know.

'Good! I'll see you on Friday, then.'

Charlie grinned at her as he prepared to shake the reins. The horse anticipated his action and began to step out. Charlie nodded his head over his shoulder. 'By the way, you were going in that direction.'

Shaking the reins, he drove away with a foolish grin on his face. If anyone had asked him what had put it there, he would have told them it was because he had just arranged to walk out with the girl he was going to marry.

Friday dawned, bright and sunny. The family had departed the previous day and, with fewer jobs to do, the servants rushed through their work at indecent speed. After a hasty lunch, the five girls set off up Chapel Lane. Goldie, in a rare moment of friendliness, readily linked arms with Ellen and Agnes, letting Doris and Patty run and skip in front of them as they joined the throngs of people who were making this annual pilgrimage up their very own 'green hill'. In spite of the solemnity of the day, there was an air of festivity. It was an extra day off work and everyone was making the most of it.

Ellen tingled with anticipation. She was going to see Charlie! Did Miss Sarah feel like this whenever she knew Mr Fairchild was coming? She didn't seem to, but then, the upper classes were trained to conceal their feelings, weren't they?

Ellen was doing her best to hide her feelings from Goldie but gosh, it was hard. She wanted to skip and jump and laugh out loud, but managed to suppress the urge. Goldie would taunt her unmercifully. And what if Charlie didn't come?

And look at all these people! How would Charlie find her? A cold shiver ran through her heart. God wouldn't let that happen, would He?

Just in case, she sent a quick, silent prayer up to heaven, assuring God she really was thankful that Jesus had died in her place ... and would He please make sure she and Charlie met up?

A number of carts and wagons taking folk from outlying farms rumbled along the road behind them. Ellen glanced at each one, wondering if Charlie would be driving his cart, but she didn't see him.

The rough track was rising steadily up the hillside, the tower on top of the Pike getting nearer with each step. This lane skirted around the bottom of the hill itself and went on further, past Lord Lever's new bungalow with its spacious grounds and fancy gardens and over to Belmont, a village down the other side, Mr John had told her, though she had never been that far. There wasn't time in the few hours off they ever had.

'I bet I get a fella before you,' Goldie boasted, as they approached the many stalls and sideshows that lined both sides of the track and the lower part of the hill.

'Bet you don't!' Ellen played along, trying to keep her voice nonchalant.

Drifting in the air were the delicious aromas of hot cross buns, cooked sausages and toffee apples and other sweet delights. Doris and Patty darted off to gaze at the goodies on sale from the various stalls, clutching small purses of pennies that they had saved especially for this occasion.

'Keep an eye on them, Agnes,' Goldie ordered.

'Aw, why me?'

''Cos I say so!'

Agnes reluctantly trailed after Doris and Patty, leaving Ellen and Goldie to saunter round the sideshows, enjoying the sights and scents of the fair.

'Hmm! Look at him over there?' Goldie

murmured, looking at a line of young men waiting to prove their strength at the hammer-pounding. 'Now, who should go for that one?'

Ellen followed her glance. The young man in question didn't appeal to her at all, especially since she knew whom she was looking out for. However, she giggled conspiratorially. 'I think it's my turn, Goldie!'

'He'll be wasted on you. Let's toss a penny.' Goldie produced a penny from her pocket. 'You call ... I'll toss.'

'All right. Heads.'

'Tails!' Goldie called in triumph, hardly glancing at the coin. 'He's mine! Well meet back at the pigeon tower, when the fair ends. I'll see you later. Ta-ra!'

Goldie gaily waved her hand and strolled over to where the young man was about to try his strength. In spite of the chill in the air, he had stripped off to the waist, showing strong muscles in his back. Goldie provocatively positioned herself where she knew she would catch his eye. He deliberately looked her up and down as he lifted the heavy hammer, both of his arms bulging with hard muscles.

Ellen watched as the hammer descended, sending the marker soaring up to the top of the measuring pole, where it sharply clanged the bell. Whatever the stall-holder handed to the victorious young man, he held it towards Goldie, an eyebrow raised in query. Goldie took it from him, responding with a similar smile. The man shrugged himself into his shirt, draped his arm around her shoulders and they strolled away as if they had known each other for years.

Ellen watched them go, feeling at a bit of a loss for the moment. Where was Charlie? Was he here yet? What if they didn't find each other?

Two hands were placed lightly over her eyes from behind.

'Guess who?' a laughing voice demanded.

Though she squealed in alarm, she recognized the voice and her heart began to thump alarmingly. 'You scared me to death!' she exclaimed, as she twisted round and met his laughing gaze. 'Where did you suddenly spring from?'

'I noticed Goldie had her eye on George Waring, so I thought I'd wait until you were on your own.' He took hold of her hand and tucked it under his arm, beaming down at her with obvious admiration in his eyes. He seemed to tower over her and tilted her face up to his with a finger under her chin. 'Will you do me the honour of allowing me to escort you around the fair, Miss Ellen Harris?'

His smile sent a warm tingle rushing through her and, with an appreciative giggle at his formality, she bowed her head gracefully. 'Delighted, I'm sure, kind sir,' she murmured, letting her eyelashes fall over her eyes, before glancing up at him again.

Her heart was beating fast. This was the closest she had been to a boy since she had left home: other than Mr John, that is. But that didn't count. They were just friends. Now, a different sort of thrill coursed through her body, sending ripples of excitement through her.

It both thrilled and alarmed her, causing hidden memories to resurface. But Charlie wasn't like that, was he? She determinedly pushed away the disturbing thoughts and laughed happily. Oh, she was going to enjoy herself today! She just knew it!

There were swingboats to ride on; hoopla stalls and coconut shies to aim at; and boot-throwing and wrestling bouts attracting men and boys alike to try their strength and ladies and girls to watch in admiration. Her head was in a whirl.

She squealed in alarm as a fire-eater put the burning stick into his mouth and, although she had seen the trick before in previous years, she hid her face in the open front of Charlie's jacket, an action that didn't displease him. She swayed slightly and he held her close to steady her. She felt the warmth of his body through her thin cotton dress. She felt safe, protected. It excited her senses but caused her to pull away. She wasn't really ready for such close contact.

'Come on! Let's ride on the swingboats!' Charlie exclaimed, sensing her withdrawal and wanting to restore her light-heartedness. He took hold of her hand again and pulled her towards the stout wooden frame that held four 'boats'. He paid their fare and helped her to scramble up into one of them.

Ellen didn't tell him she was quite capable of getting into it by herself, as she might have done if it were Mr John who was helping her. It felt nice to be treated like a lady and she cherished the sensation of being cared for.

Charlie scrambled in opposite her and took hold of his rope, handing the other across to Ellen. 'Hold on tight! Now pull hard!'

Ellen felt reckless, not caring when she felt her hat slip from off her head as they pulled alternately at the ropes, making the 'boat' swing higher and higher. Her hat was held by its ribbons and would be kept safe. Oh, it was a grand day! The best day at the Easter fair, ever!

Charlie bought a large candyfloss to share and they laughed like little children when the sugar stuck to their noses and chins as they nibbled at it and then took it in turns to dab the corner of a hankie at each other's faces.

'There's Ellen!' Doris's voice rang out.

The three girls came running over, only to stop a few yards away to gawp at their friend, who was hand in hand with the milk lad. Her face was rosy-hued and her curls were bouncing in the afternoon sunshine.

'Where's Goldie?' Doris asked bluntly, looking from one to the other.

'She ... er ... met a friend. And I met Charlie. We've been looking round the fair together.' She felt a reassuring squeeze on her hand and knew Charlie understood her embarrassment.

Charlie doffed his cap and made a slight bow. 'Good afternoon, ladies. Doris and Patty, isn't it? And ... er...?'

'Agnes,' Agnes was swift to tell him.

'Agnes. Ah, yes. I've seen you all at the Oldfields' house.'

The three maids blushed. Fancy him

knowing their names! Not that they'd get much look in, the way Ellen was holding on to his hand.

'We're going back now,' Doris said. 'Are you coming with us?'

'Oh, n-not yet,' Ellen stammered, casting a pleading eye at Charlie. It was much too soon to be leaving. 'Have you had a go at everything? There's still plenty to do. Have you had a ride on the swingboats? It's good fun.'

Agnes shrugged her shoulders. 'We've spent our money an' we're hungry. Cook said she'd have fish cakes ready for us and buttered hot cross buns.'

Charlie dug his hand into his pocket and pulled out a few pennies. 'Here, take these. That should give you a ride each and a hot cross bun. And don't worry about Ellen. I'll walk home with her later.'

'Gosh, thanks, Charlie. We'll see you later, then. Ta-ra!'

And the three girls sped away, heading for the swingboat rides.

'That was kind of you,' Ellen approved.

Charlie grinned. 'Well, I couldn't have them whisking you away so soon, could I? Besides, I want to learn more about you.' It was true, he realized. He wanted to know everything about her; what she did all day ...

102

what she wanted from life ... her family.

They were silent for a moment and then, linking hands, began to stroll up to the top of the Pike. Ellen had been before on other Good Fridays but always in the company of the other maids, tousle-haired and laughing as they scrambled and raced to be the first to reach the tower that stood on top.

'I know you're a lady's maid,' Charlie prompted her. 'But what do you do all day?'

So Ellen told him about her duties as Miss Sarah's maid and what it was like in the rest of the house. She told him of her family at Miles Platting and how she missed them, especially Tom, the only one who was a true brother, and Jack and Herbie, whom she now felt she hardly knew, and her half-sisters, Flossie and Maud.

'And what about time off?' he wanted to know. 'How am I going to get to see you, apart from a brief glimpse when I bring the milk? That's if you want to, of course?'

Ellen nodded shyly. She did. She really did, in spite of the slight tremors of aware-ness that she was stepping into potentially dangerous ground. 'Not dangerous,' she amended to herself, not with Charlie. But it was into the region of what Zach Durban had done to her and she wasn't sure she would ever forget it.

'I have a couple of hours off in the week. I have to arrange which afternoon with Miss Sarah,' she replied, 'and we'll all be in church on Sunday morning, even though the family is away.'

'I'll see you there on Sunday, then,' he promised. 'If I rush with the milk round, I should be able to finish in time.'

They paused for breath and stood looking over the Lancashire plain. On a clear day like this, you could see all the way to Blackpool on the coast and could just make out that wonderful tall iron tower that was similar to the larger one in Paris. Mr John had once said he'd take her there one day but she doubted he ever would. They belonged in different worlds. Charlie, now, was different altogether. Working class, like she was. And she already felt completely at ease with him; and excited by the different emotions that were coursing through her.

'What else do you do, besides driving the milk cart?' she asked. 'Do you have the rest of the day off?'

Charlie laughed. 'I wish! No, we're a large farming family. I'm the youngest. Most of the others have their own farms now, so there's always plenty of work to keep me busy. Milking, mucking out the cowsheds, looking after hedges and ditches and, in summer, hay-making. There's no end to it. I'll show you where our farm is when we reach the top.'

They continued to the top of the Pike and gazed around the wonderful panoramic view. Charlie pointed out the rooftops of Lord Lever's bungalow, called Roynton Cottage and, further down, surrounded by trees, the rooftops of Rivington and Black-rod Grammar School. 'Some of my brothers went there,' he told her.

'Didn't you go there, too?'

'No, I was needed to work on my brothers' farms, so I left school when I was ten. It's not that I'm a numbskull or anything,' he hastened to add. 'In fact, I'd like to learn more about motor cars. I love fiddling with engines. A couple of my brothers now have tractors instead of horses to pull their ploughs and carts and I can strip down an engine and put it back together again as easy as anything. I like tuning them up so that they work a lot better.'

They turned towards Winter Hill and the vast moorland that stretched all the way to Blackburn to the north and Bolton in the east. Charlie pointed towards Bolton, down the slopes of Winter Hill. 'Our farm's over

105

there,' he said, 'and that's my brother Joseph's and that's our Harry's.' His arm swung round as he spoke.

Ellen couldn't tell exactly where he was pointing but it didn't matter. She sighed with contentment. Charlie made her feel special. She wished their Tom could meet him. She felt they would get on well; and she knew Charlie would be a good influence on him. Her brother didn't write much but she knew he was unhappy. He was working in the cotton mill at the bottom of their street but he hated it. If only he could get away as she had done!

The sun was losing its warmth and she knew it must be getting late. 'It's been a wonderful day,' she said. 'I don't want it to end.' It was the day she had fallen in love and no other day could ever be as special.

Charlie felt the same. 'It needn't end yet,' he said, taking her into his arms. They were on the sheltered side of the tower, hidden from view to most people. She moved closer and relaxed against him as he nestled his chin into her hair. 'We've another half hour or so.'

Ellen stood encircled in his arms, partly afraid of her awareness of his masculinity and partly wondering what it would be like to be kissed by a lad such as Charlie. Did she really want that? The shadow of Zach Durban passed over her memory and her feeling of loathing when Leslie Fairchild was near. She involuntarily shivered.

'Are you cold?'

'No. I'm just...' What could she say? That she was frightened of what kissing might lead to, and of making a fool of herself because she'd never kissed a boy before? What would he expect? Would he know that she was inexperienced and didn't know how to respond?

'Don't look so worried,' he said softly. He leaned forward and his lips touched hers, gently at first, soft and teasing. Then his mouth hardened and his arms tightened around her.

She stood quietly in his arms, enjoying the sensation of his lips upon hers. The scent of him excited her. She wanted to respond ... but again the memory of Zach Durban made her pull away. 'Charlie, don't! I can't–'

He placed a finger on her lips. 'It doesn't matter. I won't do anything you don't want me to do.' He wanted to kiss her lips, her closed eyelids, the curve of her neck. He wanted to take her in his arms and lay her down and make love to her; but he knew he mustn't. She was too special for that and he didn't want to risk frightening her. 'I only want to kiss you. We've got the rest of our lives for everything else. I'll teach you ... when you're ready.' He gently kissed her again.

His breath was sweet. She put her hands around the back of his neck and held him close. Charlie's hands had slipped down to her hips and he held her against him. He felt hard against her and she sensed a flurry of excitement deep within her, tempered again with fear.

'Did you like it?' he asked softly.

'Yes. But I think we should stop. I'm sorry.'

'It's all right, love. I said I'd stop when you wanted to. Well walk on and just talk.'

'Well, well! Look who's here!'

Ellen's heart sank. It was Goldie, arm in arm with George Waring.

'Well, you're a sly one! You kept this quiet, didn't you?' Goldie continued. 'What's she like, eh? Did she let you get your hand in her drawers?'

Ellen's face blushed hot. 'Stop it, Goldie! It's not like that!'

Goldie laughed. 'I bet it's not. Shall we swap partners? I bet me and George could teach you both a thing or two!'

'We'll stay as we are, thanks,' Charlie said lightly.

'Spoil sport!' Goldie's partner grabbed hold of Ellen's arm, pulling her forward.

Charlie pulled her back again, ducking his head as George aimed a blow at him.

'Cut it out, Waring! This is neither the time nor the place for fisticuffs!'

'Scared you'll lose, are you?' George Waring bunched his fists and made a few boxing feints. 'Come on; show us what you're made of!'

Charlie was in a dilemma. He wasn't afraid to take on George Waring but it went against his upbringing to fight in front of ladies. He wasn't aware of people gathering behind him until he saw George Waring's eyes slide sideways and, at the same time, relax his boxing stance. Charlie followed his glance and saw two of his brothers standing by.

'Break it up, lads,' Isaac advised quietly. 'This is a holy day. We'll not have you desecrating it by fighting.'

They were grown men, not boys; and of no mean stature. George Waring stepped back and draped his arm around Goldie again. He half turned, then looked back over his shoulder. 'I'll remember this, Metcalfe. You'd best watch your back when your bodyguard isn't around. Yeh, you owe me one.'

Charlie watched him slouch away round the tower. 'Sorry about that,' he apologized to Ellen, taking hold of her hand again. He made a wry grimace at his brothers. 'Thanks.'

'Glad to be of service, little brother,' Isaac said with a grin. 'Annie said you'd scrubbed up well before you came out.' He smiled appreciatively at Ellen. 'Now we know why! Nice to meet you, miss.' He touched the peak of his cap towards her as he spoke.

Ellen was amazed to see Charlie's cheeks redden. She didn't know boys blushed as well as girls.

'Yeh, well, this is a new friend of mine, Ellen Harris. These are two of my brothers, Isaac and Robert.' Introductions over, Charlie slipped his arm around her shoulders. 'Come on. I'll walk you home.'

'Shall we wait with the cart for you, Charlie-boy?' Robert asked, with a sly grin.

'No, thanks. I left one of our bicycles round the back of the Crofters. I'll be back in time for milking. See you later.'

Ellen understood his embarrassment with his brothers. She'd have felt the same if their Tom or Jack was there. She bade the two men goodbye and let Charlie lead her down the rough, grassy flank of the hill. Most of the people were now making their way homeward. The best of the day was over and the air was getting cold.

They didn't talk. They just walked with their arms around each other's waists. Ellen liked it, being hugged close. No one had hugged her for years, not even her grandma. Only her mam used to hug her. And this was different. Every so often she could feel Charlie nestling his face into her hair. She was glad she'd washed it and used some of the hair preparation she made for Miss Sarah. She turned her face towards his and they kissed again. She was getting used to it now and wasn't frightened by it. She wished they could be together like this every day. She didn't want the day to end.

When they had crossed over Chorley Old Road and turned into Chapel Lane, Charlie drew her towards the wall and leaned back against it, holding her close. They kissed again, savouring the taste of each other. A few other couples passed by, one or two calling out bawdy remarks in a good-natured way. Ellen was glad they couldn't see her blushes.

When all was silent, Charlie looked up at the sky. 'The stars will be out soon. I wish we could stay out long enough to see them.

We could pick one of our very own, so that when we're apart, we'll know the other is looking at the same star.'

'Mmm. My grandma always told me to reach up for the stars,' Ellen remembered. 'She said anyone could be whatever they wanted to be, if they reached high enough. Do you believe that, too?'

'Aye, I do. I'm not going to stay a farmer's lad forever. Now I've met you, I know I'm going to follow my dream and become a motor engineer. You never know, I might even design a new car and make a name for myself like Mr Rolls and Mr Royce have done.'

Ellen didn't want to think of him moving away. She wanted him to have a dream that included her.

As if Charlie knew what she was thinking, he added, 'And you'll come with me. You'll be part of my dream from now on.'

Saturday was a busy cleaning day. Mrs Garland had heard all the gossip about Goldie and Ellen being with George Waring and Charlie Metcalfe and wasn't totally unsympathetic to the cause of 'love's young dream', as she put it.

'But I can't be letting you both have time

off together again, even though the mistress is away. You can have a couple of hours this evening, Goldie, if you get all your work done and Ellen can have some time off tomorrow afternoon, but I don't want any shenanigans from either of you, d'you hear?'

They both assured her they did, though Goldie's smirk once Cook had turned away belied her words.

Ellen didn't know what time Goldie arrived back. Bert Cadman was out, too, and as long as Goldie was home before him, there'd be no problem of being locked out. She went to bed, happily dreaming of tomorrow when she'd see Charlie after church.

Sunday dawned beautifully. The sun streamed through the attic skylights upon the sleeping forms of the five servant girls. None of them had awakened at their usual hour, mainly due to the omission of Mrs Garland's daily thump on her bedroom ceiling.

Ellen stirred first. She lay quite still for a moment, revelling in the wonderful memories of Friday ... and she was going to meet Charlie again today! She shook Goldie.

'Wake up, Goldie. I'm sure we've overslept.'

'Leave me alone!' the older girl groaned in

reply. 'I feel ill.'

Ellen knew the reason for that. The room was filled with the same boozy smell that used to surround Zach Durban. 'I'm not surprised. You've been drinking. Mrs Garland'll go dotty!'

'No, she won't. She said she was going to have a lie-in today. So leave me alone.'

The other three maids soon joined Ellen in the kitchen. With no breakfasts to prepare, the girls just had a hasty bite of some bread and jam and then Ellen clamped her hat on her head and hustled the others outside. Charlie was coming! She couldn't wait. She remembered dreaming about him. Only, her dreams were a bit muddled and she wanted to feel the touch of his hands again and, who knows, maybe a little kiss, if no one was looking.

It was a brilliant morning. The hills stood clear against the blue sky and the birds sang their beautiful songs of joy, as they revelled in the warmth of the sun. Ellen's heart sang with them. The sounds of the organ and the words of the first hymn drifted out on the fresh summer air. 'Jesus Christ is risen today! Hallelujah.'

They slipped into their pew at the back and joined in the singing. Ellen didn't know if

Charlie would make it in time for the service. He had to do the milking, after all, so she wasn't perturbed when she couldn't catch sight of him whenever they stood to sing.

At the close of the service, everyone filed outside and began to disperse to their homes. The groups of servants from various establishments were always the last to emerge from the church. Ellen hurried out with them. Where would he be? Would he be right outside or would he wait by the gate?

Blinking in the bright sunshine, she looked around but her heart sank. He wasn't there. So much for promises! He hadn't come!

Six

Monday morning brought them all back to reality, broken hearts or not. Ellen heard the milk cart approaching and peered out of an upstairs window hoping to see Charlie when he delivered the milk, just in case he'd had a good reason for not turning up at church the previous day – but she didn't recognize the man who was driving the milk cart. She turned away in disappointment, so she didn't see the man had a folded note in his hand.

It was washday. From the sound of the unwelcome thuds on her ceiling, Mrs Garland was up and running on all cylinders, determined that the rest of the servants did likewise.

'We're not having the missus think she can't leave us,' she warned. 'Everywhere's to be in a spotless condition before they arrive home.'

And it was.

Miss Sarah floated around in a dream. Leslie adored her. He had said so! Snowflakes had whirled in the Derbyshire air over the weekend and he had called her his dear 'Snow Queen'. His mother approved of her. His father took delightful liberties in teasing her. Her own mother wore a satisfied smile on her face and her father bestowed indulgent smiles upon her. Sarah basked in the glow of it ... and she failed to notice the subdued manner of her maid.

Goldie noticed, though, and took great delight in teasing and tormenting Ellen. She thought of the note that she had taken from the lad who delivered the milk that morning and had since thrown onto the kitchen fire.

'To Miss Ellen Harris' was written on the front and, inside, was a neatly written letter.

Dear Ellen,

I am sorry I was unable to come to see you at church yesterday. George Waring and his pals set on me on Saturday evening and my handsome face isn't fit to be seen. I have to be content with kissing you in my dreams. I will definitely see you outside your church next Sunday. Until then, sweet dreams.

With love from Charlie.

Goldie pursed her lips. Kissing Little Miss Innocent in his dreams, eh? She'd give him something to dream about. She'd show Charlie-boy what kisses were really like!

As soon as possible after the return home from Derbyshire, John persuaded Leslie to open up the bonnet of his motor car. He was full of eager questions, touching this and that with reverent fingers.

Leslie stood back, watching the younger man with a degree of amusement. 'My man takes care of the engine,' he admitted airily, fastidiously wiping some of the black oil off his hands onto a white lawn handkerchief. He scowled at his lack of success.

John laughed. 'Come with me. I know how to get that off.' He led Leslie round the side of the house to the kitchen entrance, walking in without knocking with the easy familiarity of one used to entering that way.

Mrs Garland looked up from her work. 'Now, Mr John, what can I do for you? Oh, I'm sorry, sir.' The sight of Mr Fairchild sent her into a flurry of action. She bobbed a hasty curtsey and began to wipe her hands on her apron.

John waved his hand at her. 'No, no, don't let us interrupt your work, Mrs Garland. I know where to find everything.'

Ellen entered the kitchen, coming for Miss Sarah's tray of afternoon tea.

Mrs Garland seized upon her entry. 'There you are, Ellen. Get the hand-cleaning stuff from under the sink for Mr John and Mr Fairchild. And, Patty, get some clean rags from the cupboard. Doris and Agnes, come with me to get some things from the cold store.'

Ellen did as she was bid, clearing a place at the sink for them.

John smiled, delighted to see her. 'I've just been tinkering with Leslie's car,' he explained, as if it was the most natural thing in the world to confide in his sister's maid. 'It was amazing to be travelling so fast. I've been looking at the engine. It's incredible.

Everything seems so small when you compare it to the size of the steam trains, yet the power is there.'

He went into some technical details, which rather went beyond Ellen's understanding but she continued to listen as she ran some hot water into a bowl for them, uncomfortably conscious of Mr Fairchild's evident interest, his eyebrows arched. As she reached over to pull the jar of soft soap towards them, she was shocked to feel her bottom pinched. She whirled around indignantly.

John was already rubbing his hands with the soap-gel, whereas Mr Fairchild was openly smirking at her. She slammed the soap jar down on the draining board.

'If that is all, I'll get on with my work,' she snapped. She grabbed hold of the tray that Doris had set for her and ran out of the kitchen.

John looked at her fleeing figure in some surprise. Leslie nudged his arm. 'You're well in there, aren't you, old boy?' he murmured. 'Quite a little dark horse, is that one.'

John looked at him sharply. 'What d'you mean?'

Leslie wiped his hands on a cloth. 'I saw her in town last week, with a farmer's lad. I bet he gets to roll her in the hay, what?'

'I shouldn't think she's ready for that sort of thing,' John protested, shocked by the crude suggestion.

Leslie winked conspiratorially. 'They're always ready. If they're keen enough, they'll find a way.' He rubbed his hands again and dropped the cloth to the floor. 'I'd say she's ready, all right.'

John felt disconcerted. He hadn't thought of Ellen in that sort of light. She was too young for that sort of thing. Or was she? He mentally counted up. She must be seventeen ... eighteen ... something like that. Good heavens! She was almost the age of Edward Cholmondeley's sister, who had tantalized him with her charms on his last visit there! And Ellen was every bit as attractive.

Leslie playfully aimed a light punch at John's chest. 'Some good sport there, what!'

John grinned weakly. He didn't want to seem too priggish to his future brother-in-law and the two young men left the kitchen laughing at further ribald comments.

'Well, well! If it isn't Harris, the shy little maid!' Leslie Fairchild put down his teacup and leaned back in his chair.

It was late teatime on the Monday afternoon. Ellen had seen Miss Sarah on her way into her mother's bedroom to ask her opinion on some of the new fashions in clothing that were becoming popular with the motoring fraternity. She had slipped into the sitting room to clear away the remnants of the afternoon tea, expecting the room to be empty. Instead, Mr Fairchild was there, leaning back in the chair with his legs extended in front of him.

Ellen paused on the threshold, stopping the door from swinging closed behind her.

'Have you come to see if you can be of any service to me? How thoughtful. Come over here, m'dear.' He indicated the space by his chair.

Ellen stepped forward reluctantly. She kept her voice impersonal as she spoke. 'Yes, sir? What can I do for you?'

He raised an eyebrow. 'You can start by coming closer, Harris. I am not accustomed to shouting my conversations across the room, especially to a serving wench.'

She moved forward again, regarding him guardedly.

'Well, Harris, you may pass me another slice of that delicious chocolate cake.'

She approached the small side table, trying not to let him know how much he unnerved her. She deftly cut a slice of the cake and slid it onto the plate.

'Would you like some cream, sir?' She gestured the jug of cream towards the plate.

He made a slight assenting movement with his head, appraising the line of her figure as she leaned towards him. 'That's enough. Mustn't be too naughty, must we?' With a quick movement, his hand grasped her wrist as she put the cream jug down onto the table.

A shudder of revulsion ran through her.

Fairchild laughed and released his hold. 'You're a bit jumpy, aren't you? Now, stand a little closer ... and stay there.'

He waited in silence until she stepped closer. Then he scooped up a portion of the cake with the cake fork and waved it towards her. 'From now on, Harris, we'll be seeing a lot more of each other, now that your mistress is almost engaged to me. I think it's time we got to know each other a little better. Don't you?'

She didn't reply. She didn't want to know this man any more than she already did. 'Will that be all, sir?'

His eyes narrowed. 'No, not yet. I might need you again when I am finished.' He leaned back once more and calmly lifted the plate onto his chest. He slowly spooned the cake into his mouth, keeping his eyes fixed on her face. The few days away in the presence of his parents and the Oldfields had given him no opportunities for any fun and games. His 'intended' barely let him touch her arm, let alone any other part of her, and he was eager to make up the deficit. Goldie would bring him some satisfaction later, but that dalliance was growing stale. He liked a bit of rough play; and genuine fear excited him. He could sense it now.

After the last crumb had been consumed, he picked up his napkin and fastidiously wiped his lips, ending with a meticulous wipe each way along his moustache. 'Perhaps I should start to call you Ellen? You wouldn't mind, would you?'

She would indeed mind. She had no desire whatsoever to hear her name on his lips.

'As you wish, sir. But I don't think Mrs Oldfield would approve of you doing so.'

'You think not? There are other things Mrs Oldfield wouldn't approve of, aren't there, Ellen? I saw you talking with a common farming lad in town, the other day. Does Mrs Oldfield know you are keeping company with such a person?'

Ellen didn't respond.

'Well?'

'No. And I'm not. That is–'

Ellen clamped her lips together. Her talking to Charlie had nothing to do with this man. She wasn't going to let him rile her.

'I shall tell her, of course ... out of deep concern for your welfare, you understand ... unless you could persuade me to keep silent, that is. We could have some fun together, you and I. I am quite generous with those who please me, you know. Ask Goldie.'

Standing to his feet, he dropped the napkin onto the floor. 'That's all, for now. Do think about my proposition, won't you?' With a casual wave of his hand, he departed and quietly closed the door after him.

Ellen shuddered. She realized she was trembling. Would he really tell Mrs Oldfield or Miss Sarah about her talking to Charlie? Not that there was anything to tell, now. As for his 'proposition'? Not even if her job depended on it! She wished she had never tracked him down that day last summer.

Later that day, Ellen was returning some ironed clothes to Miss Sarah's room when Mr John came out of his own room. He had obviously been waiting for her.

'Ellen, I'm glad I've caught you.' He glanced up and down the landing. 'You disappeared rather suddenly from the kitchen earlier. Did I do something to upset you?'

He watched her face as she considered his words. By Jove, Leslie was right! She had grown up, quite considerately so, in the past months. How was it he hadn't noticed? They'd been playmates, almost. She'd been a closer pal than his sister!

'No. I was busy, that's all,' she said at length.

'Are you sure?' He smiled disarmingly. 'What with knowing you all these years, I feel we are friends. Don't you?'

'Yes, Mr John. But, don't forget, I'm also a servant.'

He wished she didn't call him 'Mr'. It put a barrier between them. He touched her arm. 'You would tell me if there was anything wrong, wouldn't you? You don't seem to be your usual cheerful self.'

She hesitated. 'I'm just a bit tired. We had a busy time cleaning whilst you were away.'

'You did have some time off, though, didn't you? You went to the fair?'

'Yes, we went to the fair.'

John frowned. He still felt some concern but didn't know what to say. Fairchild's comments about her made him feel awkward, so he stepped aside. 'I must let you get on with your work. I just wanted to be sure we were still friends.'

He watched as she continued along the landing to his sister's room. More than likely, it was Sarah who had caused Ellen's subdued mood. He finally shrugged and turned away. Only a saint would stay cheerful all day, with her sharp criticisms ringing in their ears.

Over the next few days Ellen's natural, cheerful disposition found its way to the surface again and no one seemed to notice she hadn't been quite as buoyant as usual. She'd thought herself to be falling in love but it hadn't worked out. Were all men so unreliable? Even John seemed different towards her. Would their Tom be like that?

By the following Sunday she had put the entire Easter weekend behind her. Mr John had gone to stay with a friend from university and would return to Cambridge from there and Mr Fairchild seemed to have forgotten his threat to speak of her having a 'follower'. He would find it difficult to find any evidence, she thought ruefully.

The servants hurried through their usual Sunday morning routine. The breakfast dishes were quickly dispatched and the large joint of beef was put in the oven to roast. The vegetables were peeled, ready for cooking, the batter for the Yorkshire puddings was resting in the cold store, and the ingredients for an apple charlotte were weighed. There was nothing more to be done until they came home from church.

Ellen wore one of her better dresses, though she pushed away any thoughts that suggested she had a lingering hope that Charlie might turn up this week! And, if he did, she would simply ignore him!

She wore the shawl her mam had given her all those years ago when she left home. It was more her size now and she liked to imagine that it still had the lingering fragrance of her mam's cheap scent. It didn't ... and today its bland anonymity made her feel homesick.

By the time the servants arrived in church, the Oldfield family were already seated in their pew near the front, with Mr Fairchild beside Miss Sarah, whose face was blossoming like a rosebud unfurling its petals. Ellen felt a twinge of jealousy; she knew how her mistress felt. It had been the same for her only last week.

At the end of the service, she kept her eyes fixed firmly straight in front of her as the Oldfield party swept down the aisle. Ellen hoped they wouldn't notice that Goldie wasn't with them. The older girl had whispered something to Doris and then slipped outside during the last hymn. By the time the servants emerged into the bright sunshine, many of the day's worshippers had already departed and there was no time for the servants to linger. They had to hasten home to be sure that Sunday lunch was going according to plan.

'Where's Goldie?' Cook asked sharply.

'She's gone to talk with a friend,' Doris told her. 'She said she'll catch us up.'

'She'd better!' Cook warned. 'Come on, the rest of you. Lunch won't get itself ready!' Cook and Bert hurried off with no delay, with the four girls following. Just as they reached the Oldfields' home, they heard a shout and turned to see Goldie running down the hill towards them. They waited until she caught up with them, looking pleased with herself.

'What are you grinning at?' Ellen asked.

'Wouldn't you just like to know?' Goldie goaded her. 'I might tell you ... later!'

The afternoon passed quietly. Mr Fairchild had taken Mr and Mrs Oldfield and Miss Sarah for a spin in his motor car and they were staying out for tea, giving everyone some extra free time.

'Enjoy it whilst you can,' Bert warned. 'It's likely to be taken off us at some other time.'

Ellen chose to sit outside in the garden for half an hour. She took a book and went into the shade of the willow tree with her shawl around her shoulders. She was surprised when Doris joined her a few minutes later.

'What're you reading? Is it one of Mr John's books?'

Ellen showed her the cover. It was *Westward Ho!*

Doris pursed her lips. 'Has it no pictures in it?'

'Only a line drawing at the front. See?'

Doris was unimpressed. 'Goldie used to follow you out here when Mr John came home at the weekends. She was hoping to catch you kissing him or something like that, but she said you were dead boring and talking about books and things.'

'That's all we ever did. I like books. Do you ever wish you could read, Doris? I'll teach you, if you like.'

'Would you? Oh, I dunno, though. I can't see much use for it.'

Doris sat staring blankly ahead of her for a few minutes. Then she turned decisively towards Ellen. 'You're all right, you are, Ellen. I don't know why Goldie has it in for you so much. She's a right cow at times.' She paused and glanced around as if expecting someone to be eavesdropping outside the canopy of leaves. 'Listen, I've got to tell you ... only, you won't tell Goldie that I've told you, will you?'

'Tell me what?'

Doris hesitated, as if unsure how to continue now that she had begun. 'You know when Goldie left the church early this morning?'

Ellen nodded. 'Yes. Go on.'

'Well, she knew Charlie was coming and she went out to meet him. She told me not to say anything but I thought you should know.'

'You mean he came? But how did Goldie know? And why didn't she tell him I was in church? Why didn't you tell me?'

Doris looked as if she were about to cry. 'Goldie said I'd not to. She says they went round the back of the church and he kissed her!'

Ellen felt a tight lump in her throat. Damn Goldie!

'You won't tell her I've told you, will you?' Doris asked anxiously.

Ellen silently shook her head. She couldn't trust herself to speak. What was the point ... and if Charlie preferred Goldie to her, then he could have her! She didn't care!

Seven

It was Tuesday afternoon. Ellen's half-day off. She went into town to put a few shillings into the bank account Dorcas had advised her to open before she went back to Manchester. She earned six shillings a week now and managed to save over half of it, even though she had to buy her own shoes. It would never make her very rich but it was good to see the amount growing.

Fully absorbed in the open page of her bankbook, she emerged from the bank. Now, which way should she go? Trickett's Toffee Shop was one way; Adamson's Confectioners the other. Trickett's Toffee Shop won and she set off towards Lee Lane.

'Ellen! Wait!'

She looked in the direction of the voice, her heart skipping a beat. It was Charlie, waving to her from across the road. She saw him look quickly in both directions before running across towards her. With a determined toss of her head that set her hat bouncing on her curly locks, she turned on her heels and continued on her way. He needn't think he could play fast and loose with her!

Undeterred, he followed after her. 'I just called at the house. Doris told me you'd come into town, so I came after you, hoping I'd see you.'

Ellen continued along the street with her head held high. Her heart was racing and her cheeks felt very hot. Who did he think he was? And, more importantly, who did he think she was? He had a cheek, he did! To go off with another girl ... Goldie of all girls! ... and then to expect her to greet him with open arms!

She tried to ignore him, which was a bit difficult, as he was now level with her left shoulder and gave no sign of dropping back. She kept her eyes very much to the front, though she would have loved to have been able to see the effect it was having on him. Not a very significant one, if his persistent attempts at gaining her attention were anything to go by.

'I'm sorry I missed you last Sunday,' he went on, as though he were used to having a conversation with the back of someone's head, 'but I expect Goldie told you all about that.'

His open confession about Goldie did

what the rest of his words had failed to do. She stopped her headlong walk and turned to face him.

Her reproofs were stilled on her tongue by the sight of him. The left side of his face was completely covered in bruises, all shades of black, blue and yellow.

'You've been fighting!'

She couldn't help the accusing tone in her voice. Her mam always warned her not to bother with anyone who used his fists. 'He'll use them on you before you know where you are,' she'd warned. And she should know, the way Zach Durban knocked her about!

Charlie grimaced wryly.

'Aye. It was George Waring and his pals. I was a bit outnumbered. That's why I sent you that note, telling you why I hadn't made it to church on Easter Sunday. Me mam was ashamed to let me out.'

Ellen's mind was spinning.

'George Waring did that to you? Why?'

'He felt I had made him look stupid, so he got his pals to lie in wait for me on Easter Saturday night, like I told you in my note.'

'I didn't get a note from you.'

'You must have done. Harry said he'd given it a pretty girl. I assumed he meant you.'

'Well, it wasn't.'

133

The obvious name hit them both.

'Goldie!'

Another thought hit Ellen. 'What else did you say in your note?'

Charlie shrugged his shoulders. 'That I missed you and I would see you after church this Sunday instead.'

So that was why Goldie had slipped out of church early! Still...!

'You needn't have kissed her, though,' Ellen accused, still hurting at the thought of it.

Charlie shrugged again, looking shame-faced. 'Well, you know Goldie. She came dashing out of church and beckoned to me to follow her. I thought she was taking me to you. Then she said that you hadn't gone to church that morning and that you didn't want to see me again. Before I knew what she was doing, she'd grabbed hold of me and was kissing me.'

'Huh! You could have stopped her.'

'She took me by surprise. It didn't mean anything, anyway. She's not my type. Girls like Goldie are two a penny. You're different.' His eyes softened and he reached out to touch her arm. 'Did you think I had deserted you? As if I would, after the kisses we shared!'

Ellen felt her cheeks reddening at the

reference to those magical moments when his lips had touched hers. Her lips tingled now at the remembrance, longing to repeat the sensation.

Charlie drew her closer and their lips met. For a few wonderful moments, Ellen melted into his embrace, returning his kisses, forgetting they were on a public street until she heard a woman who was passing by say, 'Ugh! How disgusting! I don't know what the world is coming to!'

Embarrassed, Ellen pulled away. She remembered her resolve not to be so easily taken in again, but she wanted to believe him. The very nearness of him dissolved any bitterness that she had felt towards him. She loved him. You had to trust the one you loved, didn't you!

As if he knew what she was thinking, Charlie grasped hold of her hands. 'I'm sorry you thought I'd deserted you. I really thought Goldie had a message from you. I told her to tell you I'd come to the house today. I should have guessed she wouldn't!'

'Then, it's a good thing it was Doris you saw or Goldie might have convinced you I really didn't want to see you again.'

'Does that mean you do want to?'

Ellen nodded and linked her arm with his.

'Yes. I've been miserable without you.'

The early weeks of that summer flew by.

'I wish you were all in love,' Cook quipped as she watched Ellen happily skip through her work. 'We'd get through all the work in no time!'

Not everyone shared Cook's admiration.

'Do you have to sing so much, Harris?' Miss Sarah snapped, drawing the back of her hand across her brow. 'I have a headache and I would recover much faster if I could have some silence. Dampen this cloth again, will you! And draw the curtains closer. The light hurts my eyes.'

'Yes, Miss Sarah,' Ellen agreed, complying with good humour. She hummed under her breath until she was on her own again. Her happiness was too wonderful to keep it bottled up.

'Anyone would think he was someone special!' Goldie later taunted. 'He's only a farm-boy. Not Prince Charming!'

'Ooh, he's got a lovely smile, though,' Doris admired. 'I wish I had someone who looked at me like that.'

'He's smiling because he's working out how he's going to get into her drawers today,' Goldie informed her. 'He won't smile for long, if she keeps him out!'

'You should wash your mouth out with soap, you should,' Doris replied. 'You'd best not let Cook hear you talking like that.'

'Cook's a dried-up prune,' Goldie said carelessly. 'What would she know? I bet she's never had a man panting round after her! She wouldn't know what to do with one if she had. Come to that, Ellen hasn't got a much better idea herself, have you?'

'Mind your own business and I'll mind mine!' Ellen snapped. It was her afternoon off and she had plans in her head – and she wasn't going to tell the others until she had accomplished them.

She was going to persuade Charlie to teach her how to ride his bicycle and then she would get one of her own so that they could go further afield on her few hours off.

Charlie agreed and they went up George's Lane, where people were few and far between on a day like this. With the front of her skirt pulled back through her legs and the back portion pulled forwards, Ellen spent a number of wobbly hours mastering the technique, accompanied by squeals and shrieks as the bicycle seemed to make up its own mind where to go. It was such fun! Especially when she fell off the bike into Charlie's arms, giving them more opportunities to kiss.

They lay on a grassy bank side by side, looking up at the small white clouds scudding across the sky. It was so easy to talk ... mostly. Ellen thought her heart was going to stop beating when Charlie asked her diffidently if some lad had 'hurt' her at some time. Her cheeks burned with shame, but she couldn't tell him. She just couldn't! The memory still filled her with shame. He might think she had encouraged her stepfather. He wouldn't know how vile he was! It made her feel dirty, just thinking about him!

Charlie tickled her with a long-stemmed grass, distracting her from her unpleasant thoughts. All too soon the afternoon was over and, laughing merrily, they sped back down Chapel Lane. It was as well that their arrival back at the Oldfield house went unnoticed. Miss Sarah would have been quite horrified to see her maid with her skirt drawn up to her knees, held closely in place on the crossbar by her farm boy's strong arms, her hair blown back in his face.

The magical summer danced on.

Ellen withdrew some of her savings and bought a bicycle from Frank Hart's bicycle shop and she and Charlie cycled the country lanes around Rivington; other days they walked arm in arm round Lord Lever's Park, admiring the zebras, emus, yaks and the other wild animals that grazed there.

They talked, laughed and made plans for the future. If it rained on Sundays or Tuesdays, they barely noticed. They found a teashop just off Scholes Bank, where they could linger over a pot of tea and raspberry buns, talking and planning, their lives spreading out in front of them.

One such Tuesday, Charlie was filled with enthusiasm. 'Rolls-Royce, that car manufacturing company I told you about in the Midlands, has brought out a new car. It's got real class. It's called the Silver Ghost. Only the top brass will be able to afford it.' He dropped his eyes for a moment, and gave an impatient sigh. The engineers are improving standards all the time. It makes me want to get down there and be part of it all. I feel, I don't know, more alive, I suppose, when I'm tuning up engines. I want to do more than just work with the tractors on the farm.'

Ellen nodded. 'I know how you feel. I don't want to be a lady's maid all my life. I feel I can do more. I talk with John ... Mr John, you know ... about politics and such. It's exhilarating when we argue about it.

Times are changing and I want to change with it. But I don't know how.'

'The only way is to go where it's all happening. For me, that's down in the Midlands. I sometimes think there'll be nothing left for me to do by the time I get there.'

Ellen's heart skipped a beat but she kept a smile on her face. 'Maybe your father will let you go a bit sooner, if you ask him,' she suggested, though inwardly she felt a cold shiver clasp icy fingers around her stomach. She didn't want him to go. She wanted him to stay here, with her.

Charlie shook his head. 'It would have to be a good offer. They need me on the farms. Mind you, they know I'll go someday, but I don't want to go against their wishes.'

'I don't like thinking about you going away. I don't want to lose you.'

'Who's talking of you losing me? I hope you'll be coming with me.'

'Is that a proposal?'

'Sort of,' Charlie replied, 'though I can't afford to get married yet.' He reached across the table and picked up her hand. 'Are you willing to wait to marry me?'

She needed no time for thought. 'Yes. I'll wait as long as it takes.'

The summer rushed on. July gave way to August. The annual church outing took place on the afternoon of the third Saturday. The picnic was to be held in the grounds of Rivington Hall Barn, one of two old tithe barns that Lord Lever had restored to provide refreshments for visitors to his park. Most of the congregation looked forward to their ride in Livesey's huge, horse-drawn wagonette. It had to make three journeys, crammed full of parishioners seated on six rows of wooden benches.

Canon Garret had delegated most of the organizing of setting up trestle tables and other such jobs to his parish council but his wife was efficiently in charge of the clusters of female servants who were covering the tables with pristine white cloths and spreading out trays of food, ready for when the more genteel parishioners arrived. Those who wished could partake of their afternoon tea inside the Hall Barn but most of them preferred the excitement of an outdoor picnic.

Charlie was busy hay-making on the farm belonging to one of his many brothers. He had warned Ellen that late summer was a very busy time. She didn't really want to go to the picnic without him but everyone else was going, even the Oldfield family. And Charlie promised to get there later if he were able to do so.

The Oldfields arrived in Mr Fairchild's motor car, having left home later than the wagonettes. Miss Sarah looked extremely pretty in a pale, pink afternoon dress. More than one young lady eyed her with envy as she strolled from the motor car to the selection of chairs set out under the trees, twirling a matching pink parasol over her large picture hat.

The scent of freshly mown grass lay heavy in the warm air. Bees and butterflies swooped and hovered, their tiny wings beating a frantic tune that made humans feel drowsy, their eyelids heavy. Many of the older ones rested their eyes for a few minutes, but not so the younger ones. There were too many exciting things to be doing. Time to sleep would come later.

Charlie's absence left Ellen free to help with some of the little ones, whose parents were glad enough to relinquish their responsibilities for a few hours. She found herself partnered with John in organizing some of the races. Family times like this always made her wish her own younger brothers and sisters could have been there. What a difference it would make to their drab lives.

'Oh! I'm exhausted,' she said with a laugh, dropping down onto a grassy bank on the fringe of the revelries, when someone else took over for the older children.

'I'll get you a drink,' John offered. 'Don't go away.'

She watched him thread his way through the crowds of children to the refreshment table that some of the ladies were managing. With a contented sigh, she lay back against the warm grass. Buttercups and clovers tickled her face as the warm breeze wafted them gently, disturbing their laden pollen. Aware that someone had sat down beside her, she lazily opened her eyes, expecting to see John.

Mr Fairchild's mocking face startled her.

She immediately made a move to scramble to her feet but Mr Fairchild grasped hold of her hand, forcing her to remain on the grass.

'Don't run away, m'dear. I noticed your gallant escort desert you and decided to come to keep you company until he returns. I think it's time we became friends. Don't you? Especially since I haven't reported your dalliances with your farmer's lad to Mrs Oldfield. I deserve some sort of recompense for that, don't you think?'

Ellen cast urgent glances around. Where was John? Who could she call out to?

'Leave me alone,' she hissed, not wanting to cause a scene.

'I could advance your position,' he continued, ignoring her refusal. 'That is, if you were a little more friendly ... towards me. You seem to be a bright girl. You must see the advantages of a "patron". I could set you up somewhere nice. What d'you say?'

She tried to pull her hand away but his grip tightened. His nearness repelled her.

He smiled at her with the ease of one used to charming the ladies. He cut quite a figure in his tailor-made casual suit, his straw boater cast down on the grass beside him. To a casual observer, they would appear to be having a quiet conversation.

Ellen was unable to take her eyes off the moustache adorning his top lip. For some reason, it reminded her of two slugs, meeting together under his nose. If she hadn't felt so full of loathing, she would have laughed at the thought.

A white butterfly carelessly alighted onto a nearby stem of grass. With a swift scooping movement, he trapped it in his hand. 'I could hold you, as gently as I am holding this fragile creature,' he offered.

Ellen felt her glance dragged down to his hand in reluctant fascination. 'Don't...!'

'On the other hand, if you continue to make me angry...' He slowly squeezed his finger tightly against his palm, and then let the mangled remains of the butterfly fall to the grass, flicking his thumb across his fingers for a number of times, to remove the traces of the white scales.

Ellen felt revulsion well up inside her. It broke the spell and she scrambled to her feet.

'Think about it, m'dear. There's plenty of time.' He lay back on the grass, his hands clasped behind his head, smiling up at the sky as she gathered her skirt around her and ran towards the refreshment tables.

'Hey! Where are you off to? Did you think I wasn't coming back?'

She halted, realizing that John was standing in front of her with two glasses of lemonade in his hands.

'Here, hold these for a minute. I'll get some cakes.' He thrust them into her hands and disappeared into the melee once more. Within a minute, he was back at her side. 'Come on; let's sit under that tree over there. Are you all right? You look a bit pale.'

'I'm all right. It's just...' What could she say? She couldn't find adequate words to express how she felt. Her hands were shaking. 'Let's join that group of young people over there. Your mother wouldn't like us to be sitting alone.'

'My mother doesn't like a lot of my ways,' he laughed. 'I sometimes enjoy shocking her. Haven't you noticed?'

His blasé attitude made her feel angry. 'You're her son. I'm only a servant. She could sack me, if she wanted to.'

John seemed startled by her anger. 'I don't think of you as a servant. More as a friend, really. One day soon all this "class" business will change. It's bound to. Working-class people want more from life than pure drudgery.'

'Do you think it will change in our lifetime?' Ellen asked wistfully.

John shrugged. 'I don't know. It would need something pretty earth-shattering to break down the barriers that quickly. It could take years. Look how long it took to get slavery abolished.' He grinned impishly at her. 'I tell you what, when I have my own establishment, you shall come and run it for me and, between us, we'll have no distinction of class!'

Nevertheless, when it was time to return home, John departed with the rest of his family in Mr Fairchild's motor car, leaving Ellen, with the other servants, to await their turn in the wagonette. Like it or not, the difference was still there ... and probably always would be.

Charlie continued to be in great demand on his brothers' farms. Ellen would have loved to join him, perfectly sure that she would fit in and enjoy the manual labour. He had told her that all the women helped – and the children. A fine day missed could mean a harvest lost. But the distance was too great to make the journey there and back again in her off-duty hours, so she had to be content to wait until it was all over. However, when the end of the harvest came, it wasn't the pleasure she expected it to be.

There was to be a barn dance, at one of the nearby farms. Different farmers hosted this event each year. This year, it was held at Higher Meadows Farm. The large barn that housed the machinery was cleared; straw bales were placed around to provide some of the seating; and coloured streamers and flags decorated the building. All the farmers' wives provided large dishes of hotpot, fresh bread, butter, cheeses and a variety of pickles to accompany it all. A generous supply of various home-brewed ales was gathered and the whole event was generally acclaimed to be the highlight of the year.

Ellen traded her Tuesday afternoon off for the Saturday evening, plus a little extra time out of Mrs Garland's generosity ... as long as she was up at the usual time on the Sunday morning. She bought a pretty white cotton top, fastened at the front with white laces, to wear with one of her off-duty skirts. She felt excited and happy, as she waited for a wagonette to come to pick her up.

As soon as she saw Charlie, she knew that something exciting had happened. He looked fit to burst but wouldn't be drawn. 'I'll tell you later,' he promised, kissing her lips lightly. 'Come on. Let's join in the dancing.'

Ellen soon picked up the sequences of the dances and skipped and twirled with the rest of them. She was in Charlie's arms and that was all that mattered. She couldn't take her eyes away from his face, suddenly feeling the need to memorize every feature and, by the look of him, neither could Charlie take his eyes from her.

Oh, she loved him so much! She felt deliriously happy! The way he held her, the way he looked at her, she wanted to melt into the midst of him and she was sure he wanted the same. But they'd wait. He'd promised her.

Charlie didn't share his news with her until they were taking a rest between dances after their supper. He pulled her down to sit beside him on a bale of hay and took both her hands in his. Somehow, before he had even begun to speak, she knew something was going to happen to change everything. It was the look in his eyes. They were full of excitement – yet held a shimmer of sadness.

'I was called over to Brownlow's farm yesterday to see if I could fix their tractor,' he began. 'They were so near the end of the harvest, they didn't want to lose time by getting someone in to have a look at it. One of Lord Lever's men was there having a go at it and said there was a big repair job needed on one of his lordship's guests' motor car. His engineers couldn't get it right. Anyway, by the time I had fixed Brownlow's tractor, he was so impressed he took me along to Lord Lever's bungalow to see if I could fix the problem with the motor car – and I did! Mr Allington, the owner of the car, came to the farm to talk to Father and, between them, they came to an agreement. Father says I can go!'

Ellen felt a chill cut through to her stomach. 'Go?' she echoed. 'Go where?'

'Down to the Midlands. Mr Allington knows the owner of a new large car-manu-facturing business. He said that he's been on the lookout for someone like me. He knows I've not had any real training but he said that it's the skill to be able to do the job that counts, not a bit of paper with words written on it. He's going to see that I get any extra training that I need.' He paused, his face flushed with excitement. 'What do you think? Isn't it a wonderful chance for me?'

Ellen swallowed hard. 'Yes. When ... when do you go?'

Charlie's expression sobered. 'He wants me to go back with him tomorrow, to start on Monday. He says every day counts, there's that much competition in the business. I know it's very short notice but this could be my big chance.' His eagerness, his enthusiasm, was pouring out of him. 'It's what I long to do ... to make motor cars ... to develop better engines. I know I can do it. I have ideas – lots of them. I want to put them into practice, to try them out.'

The pain started somewhere deep inside her and knifed its way upward, tearing her, wrenching her. She tried to ignore it. Illness and disease caused pain, not words. Charlie was smiling, trying to reassure her, but a misty haze distorted his face and his voice seemed far away. 'It will only be a short while, Ellen. I know we talked of it being in two years' time when we could get married and go away together but I can't let this chance pass me by, especially with my father saying I can go. Please say that you're pleased for me.'

She couldn't bear it. How would she manage? She pushed away her pangs of loss. It was true. It was his big chance. He had to take it. She couldn't hold him back. She forced a smile onto her lips.

'It's wonderful. Of course I'm pleased for you ... but...' She looked eagerly into his face. 'Can't I come with you?'

Charlie looked at her sadly, as he gently stroked her hand. 'Mr Allington says he can put me up for a few weeks, till I find lodgings. He says that it's easy for single young men to find a place but that it's rough on the women. The time will fly by – honestly. And we'll write to each other every week.' He laughed. 'Or every day! It'll only be a year; or eighteen months maybe. Two years at the most. I'll be earning good money by then. We'll get somewhere nice.'

'What if you meet someone else?' she whispered. 'I love you. I don't want to lose

151

you.' Her hands felt cold in his.

'You won't lose me. I love you. You know I do. Let's go outside. I want to hold you.'

They linked their fingers together, as Charlie led the way outside. He stopped and pointed up to the darkening sky. 'Remember, the same stars will be twinkling over Birmingham. Choose one ... then that one will be ours. Which shall we choose?'

Ellen looked, though she couldn't really make out any individual stars, her eyes were brimming with unshed tears. 'That bright one,' she said, pointing to the sky. 'The brightest star will be ours ... then we'll always be able to see it.'

Charlie squeezed her hand. 'That's my girl!' He kissed her lips, tasting her salty tears. 'Come on, let's find somewhere private.'

Other farm buildings were nearby. They found one with fresh, dry hay piled up towards the roof. Charlie held out his hand to assist Ellen to scramble up after him. They settled on a ledge of hay, about halfway up the barn. Charlie stamped around a bit to level it off, then gently pulled Ellen down beside him. 'I love you. There'll never be anyone else for me, no matter how far away I go or how long I may be away. Promise me that you'll wait for me.'

'I'll wait but I don't know how I'm going to bear it,' she sobbed. 'I love you so much, Charlie.'

Charlie drew her towards him and feverishly kissed her, all over her face and down her neck. His hands stroked her hair back from her face and he buried his face in the sweet-scented curls.

Her heart skipped a beat as his hands travelled down her body. Instinctively, she arched towards him, her breasts straining at the bodice that she wore next to her skin. His fingers nimbly undid the row of buttons and then the laces that held her cotton top together. He pressed his face into the valley between her firm young breasts. 'You're lovely,' he murmured. 'Did you know?'

She shook her head shyly. 'No,' she whispered. 'Tell me.'

He cupped his hands around her face and nudged his nose against hers. 'You are beautiful. Your eyes, your hair, your cheeks, your nose.' He traced his lips over her as he spoke each word, leaving a trembling trail behind him. 'Your neck ... and down here.' His kisses led down to her breasts, sending a shaft of molten fire down her body to her most secret place.

She was intoxicated by his kisses. Her

body revelled in his caresses, though her heart was breaking in the anguish of his near departure. She didn't want him to go. She needed him. She wanted him to be part of her. As his hands drew up her skirt, she felt that she was overtaken by a sense of reckless abandon. Her body curved into his, stimulated by his touch. Their kisses increased in fervour. Their passion intensified.

His movement, as he rolled on top of her, broke the enchantment.

Suddenly, it wasn't Charlie, who was on top of her, but Zach Durban, her stepfather. Her body stiffened. 'Charlie, don't.'

'Shh! I won't hurt you.' He lowered his head again and ran his tongue over her breasts, delighting in the taste of her.

A tremor ran through her ... not of pleasure, but of fear. 'No! No! I can't! You mustn't!'

'I love you! It'll be all right.' His voice was tender.

She pushed at his chest and wildly rolled away, her agitation adding strength to her muscles. She gathered her skirt and scrambled to the edge of the hay.

Charlie hadn't moved. It had happened so quickly. Only now did he try to persuade her not to run away. 'Ellen! Don't go! It doesn't matter! Wait for me!'

She didn't stop. She slithered down the bales of hay, collecting scratches that she would only be aware of later. On reaching ground level, she held the open front of her cotton top together and ran out of the barn. People were leaving the dance. She careered into two young men, who tried to steady her, but she whirled away, hearing them laugh behind her.

Music still poured out of the barn. Happy bursts of laughter and friendly banter filled the air. Some people were calling out for their transport; drivers called their destinations.

She stood in the shadows, her breath bursting out in short gulps, as she quickly fastened up the laces that Charlie had so lovingly undone and then headed towards the wagonettes. Someone recognized her and reached out a helping hand. She was hauled aboard as the wagonette lurched forwards. No one noticed her quietness. They were too busy exchanging their comments on the evening's fun or enjoying a quiet kiss in the darkness.

She looked back, as the wagonette rumbled out onto the road. The music was fading away, the lights becoming dimmer. She wasn't sure if she saw Charlie. She had the impression of him stumbling out of the barn, calling her name, standing in the cool night air, wondering where she had gone, scratching his head in bewilderment when he couldn't find her.

The wagonette turned the corner and her eyes stared into the darkness. When would she see him again?

Eight

April 1909

'Not there, Harris! Sweep it up higher! I want the diamonds to be seen from the front, as well as from behind.'

Miss Sarah's voice rose high in her exasperation. She was nervous – far more nervous than she had ever been in her life. All those people were here to see her, Miss Sarah Oldfield, spinster – how she hated that word! – of this parish, take that first wonderful step towards being free of that emotionally frigid description.

Oh, she knew what they all said. Cold, haughty, devoid of feeling. But she wasn't! Not deep inside! She did have feelings – she simply couldn't express them. Conscious of her mama's teachings, she had always felt unable to respond to the tentative overtures from the short string of vetted young men who had been paraded before her – until dear Leslie appeared on the scene. He had changed her life. He had persisted, where other would-be suitors had swiftly withdrawn. And, tonight, everyone would see her as she really was! The delight of a handsome young man's eye!

Her heart fluttered wildly. No one, not even dear Mama, had fully known of her dread of being left on the shelf. One by one her friends and acquaintances had announced their engagement, slyly gloating over her discomfort, she knew. Well, now she could join their privileged band. No longer would they cease their conversations of matters appertaining to marriage whenever she joined them, smiling secret smiles. By the end of this year, she would be privy to it all – she would understand that beguiling secret that the married ladies of her acquaintance would only speak of behind fluttering fans. She sighed contentedly. Tonight was her engagement ball.

In the time-honoured way, Leslie had proposed to her on bended knee and she had accepted. And now, after weeks of planning and countless visits to Whitaker's show-rooms in Bolton, she was dressed divinely in a powder-blue gown. In a few moments, Papa would be coming to escort her down the magnificent sweeping staircase into the ballroom of Bolton Town Hall – and she wouldn't be ready!

'Do hurry, Harris! Time is pressing!'

'Yes, Miss Sarah,' Ellen replied, lifting the pompadour about half an inch higher, teasing out the pad of combings, to achieve a fuller style. 'How does this look?'

'Much better. And do make sure that the larger diamond is exactly at the centre back. I want it to look absolutely perfect.'

'You look wonderful, Miss Sarah.' Ellen removed the cotton cape, which she had placed around her mistress's shoulders to protect her silk gown from any make-up powder. 'Now, just take a look in the long mirror, Miss Sarah. What do you think?'

Miss Sarah stood before the long mirror and slowly turned round, looking at her reflection with a critical air. She turned from side to side, holding her breath.

It was true. She did look wonderful. Thousands of tiny sequins had been hand-sewn into place on the chiffon overskirt of her gown; long, pale-blue kid gloves encased her arms; and tiny blue feathers, mingling with diamonds, adorned her hair. Leslie would be the envy of every man present.

Moments later, Ellen and Goldie, concealed in the shadows of the long velvet curtains on the balcony, listened to the soft gasps of approval as Mr Oldfield escorted his daughter down the magnificent staircase and handed her to her new fiancé. A ripple of applause greeted the newly engaged couple as they proceeded between their guests to the centre of the ballroom. The musicians began to play and the couple waltzed around the room, the diamonds in Miss Sarah's hair shimmering in the reflected light from the crystal chandeliers.

Flowers were everywhere. Their scent filled the ballroom and drifted up to the landing, where the two maids watched the dancing couples in silence for a while. Time and again, the music faded, the dancers dispersed and a happy babble of conversation rose up to the enthralled spectators on the balcony. Time seemed to stand still.

A pang of jealousy struck Ellen's heart. Why couldn't her romance with Charlie progress like this? Oh, nothing so grand! That wasn't what she meant! Never a day went by without her thinking of him; never an evening that she didn't look up at the stars and wonder if Charlie was looking at them also. He hadn't written many letters, even though he had promised to. He–

'Look out! Miss Sarah's on her way up the stairs!' Goldie warned, breaking into her reverie.

Ellen shot back into the powder room, ready to welcome Miss Sarah.

'I need my fan, Harris. You forgot to give it to me. You did bring it, didn't you?'

'Yes, Miss Sarah. Here it is. Shall I touch up your make-up, whilst you are here?'

'Not yet. We will be going in for supper soon. I will need you straight afterwards, to renew my lipstick.'

'Very well, Miss Sarah. I'll be here.'

Ellen watched her descend to the glittering ballroom. Mr Fairchild wasn't in sight. However, a friend of Miss Sarah's attracted her attention from down below and Miss Sarah went down to join her.

The musicians struck up for a waltz and the floor gradually filled. She saw Mr Oldfield lead Mrs Fairchild onto the floor while Mr Fairchild senior approached Mrs Oldfield.

Goldie was nowhere to be seen. Ellen

leaned over the balustrade, searching the faces of the dancing couples for John and his partner, when his well-known voice sounded behind her.

'Miss Harris, may I have the pleasure of this dance, please?'

'Dance? I don't know how. Besides, even if I could, I couldn't dance here,' Ellen said, laughing. 'Your mother would have a fit if she saw us!'

John looked down at her. Every time he came home from Cambridge, she seemed to have grown up some more. His heart missed a beat. Her lips were parted slightly as she looked up at him. Her lips... Could lips be so red and so ... kissable? He had a sudden longing to pull her close and cover those tempting lips with his own. He bet they tasted sweeter than any he'd tasted before. His eyes travelled down her slender body. Her maid's attire revealed very little of her flesh; not like the well-dressed young ladies dancing to the music of the small orchestra downstairs. But none stirred his deep emotions as did this girl ... his sister's maid, for heaven's sake! He knew that some of his high-society friends had many a dalliance with maids in their households and, as long as they were discreet about it, no censure was brought upon them, but he hated to think of Ellen in that light.

The smile around her eyes was fading. She seemed puzzled at his silent contemplation of her. He shook his thoughts away. This was no time for seriousness. It was party time. Suddenly he felt light-hearted.

He grinned boyishly. 'No one will know.'

Ellen was bemused as he placed his right hand around her slim waist and pulled her towards him. Instinctively, she put her left hand onto his shoulder, surprised, yet elated, as his smile melted away her reservations. A warm thrill ran down her spine, as their bodies touched. John tucked her free hand into his and began to lead her carefully around the limited space, moving to the regular rhythm of the music. He pulled her closer, letting the strength of his thighs guide her as they whirled and spun as if they had practised each step.

It seemed like a dream to Ellen. The feel of his breath on her face and the delicate touch of his lips on her cheek, as he quietly hummed the melody, excited her senses. Only Charlie had ever made her feel like this. She felt confused. Why didn't he write more often? Why did her body feel like this?

The music was coming to an end. Their

movements slowed down, then accelerated again, as Mr John led her into a whirling climax that left them motionless in the shadows of the velvet curtains. Their eyes met in mutual pleasure.

'That was wonderf–'

The ending of the word was lost as John's lips descended on hers and moved lightly upon them. Although shocked, she felt an answering longing well up in the depths of her body. It had been so long since Charlie! Her lips parted a little. She wanted ... what Charlie had wanted. No, no! This wasn't Charlie! Her body stiffened; the old familiar panic coursed through her; and she squirmed free.

John took in Ellen's white face. He straightened his arms and held himself away from her. 'I'm sorry. The music ... I got carried away.' His senses were reeling. What was he thinking of? This was his sister's engagement party and here he was, wanting to hold ... to kiss ... to... He shook his head. It must be the wine, the euphoria of the atmosphere.

He saw the colour return to Ellen's face and he relaxed. It had only been a kiss. Friends exchanged kisses, especially at parties. It meant nothing. He smiled.

'That was the best dance tonight,' he exclaimed, rather more heartily than he meant to. He glanced about quickly, anxious now to lose himself in the crowd below. My, it was hot up here. His finger pulled at the front of his collar. 'I must rejoin the party.' He glanced around, thrown off balance. 'I'll ... er ... I'll bring a plate of food up to you and Goldie. I don't suppose my dear sister will think of that.'

Ellen's eyes were fixed on his. They were beautiful, like deep pools. The taste of her! But, she was right. If his mother... He lightly touched her cheek with his fingers. 'I think our dance had better be our secret, don't you?'

Ellen nodded. 'Yes.' Her lashes curled upon her cheeks, as she glanced down.

John longed to hold her again but a resounding gong echoed through the hall, announcing supper. He shrugged wryly. 'I'd better go.' He backed away, smiling ruefully, before skipping lightly down the stairs.

Ellen watched him go with her mind in turmoil. She could still feel the pressure of his youthful firmness. Her lips still tingled from his touch. She felt primed for ... what?

'But I love Charlie!' Charlie's not here! 'Charlie loves me!' How do you know? He hasn't written for weeks!

A movement behind her caused her to spin

round. Still half-hidden in the shadows, her hand flew to touch her flaming cheeks. It was Mr Fairchild. He paused, returning her startled glance, and then ran lightly down the stairs and merged in with the guests.

Goldie's voice disturbed her troubled thoughts. 'What's happening, Ellen? Was that the supper gong?'

Ellen jumped at the sound of her voice. Where had Goldie sprung from? Had she seen them dancing, kissing? No, she would have said so straight away. The thought that anyone might have seen them brought a fresh palpitation to the rhythm of her heart. She forced her voice to be steady. 'Yes. Miss Sarah said that I must stay here, ready to touch up her lipstick and powder afterwards.'

She leaned over the balustrade, pretending to be watching the guests as they went for their supper, giving the erratic beating of her heart time to settle down. Part of her felt cross at the foolishness of John's action. She would be sacked immediately if Mrs Oldfield or Miss Sarah had seen them dancing together, never mind kissing! No matter that it had been John who had initiated the intimacy of the dance and ... and afterwards!

The touch of his breath still lingered on her cheeks; the scent of his skin lingered in her nostrils, sending a fresh spasm of bewildered ecstasy coursing through her body.

But it was Charlie who held her heart in his hand! It was he who bled it dry every day when there was no word from him. It was his name she cried out in her dreams. Charlie ... not John. Charlie, write to me!

It was in the early hours of the next day that Ellen helped Miss Sarah out of her ballgown in the privacy of her own bedroom.

Miss Sarah's wonderful night had ended rather differently than she had expected when she succumbed to a temporary incapacity caused by overindulgence at the punch bowl. It had been alleviated by the indignity of her vomiting into a porcelain bowl that her ever-watchful maid had produced from off the dresser.

Ellen guided her mistress towards her bed but Miss Sarah preferred to slide to the floor. Ellen did her best to quickly remove the constricting stays and fine lace bodice that clothed the young woman. The many small buttons made the task more difficult, especially when Miss Sarah insisted on rolling over onto her back. When Mrs Oldfield came into the room, dressed in her satin nightrobe and negligee, Ellen was relieved to discover that she had come to help to get her daughter into bed. Together, they managed to remove the rest of her clothing and slip her nightgown over her head, before letting her sink into her much-needed sleep.

'I trust that you will be very discreet about the details of Miss Sarah's incapacity this evening, Harris,' Mrs Oldfield challenged Ellen.

Ellen met her eyes. 'Of course, ma'am. No one need know any more than that the excitement of the evening was too much for her.'

'Precisely, Harris. Now, if you will just put away Miss Sarah's jewellery, you may retire to your room.'

Ellen gratefully tidied the top of the dressing table and picked up the diamond tiara, necklace and earrings that had adorned Miss Sarah that evening.

'Not that box,' Mrs Oldfield intervened. 'I have given her a new box to keep her diamonds in. You will find it in the top right-hand drawer.'

Ellen quickly located it. It was a beautifully carved walnut box, with a small key in its lock. Ellen turned the key and opened the lid. The box wasn't empty. She stared at its contents.

'What is the matter, girl? Get on with it.'

Ellen couldn't speak. She held out the box towards Mrs Oldfield. There, in one of the places specially designed to hold rings, was a beautiful diamond ring, the centre of which was shaped like a star – the ring that had caused Nora's dismissal two and a half years previously.

Mrs Oldfield stared into the box, her face turning as white as Ellen's. 'I don't understand, Harris,' she eventually admitted, her face twitching, as she urged her reluctant brain to consider the matter.

Ellen waited.

'Maybe Miss Sarah bought another ring to replace the one that went missing? It was her favourite ring at the time,' Mrs Oldfield suggested. 'Or maybe Mr Fairchild bought it for her? Yes, that is what has happened. You needn't concern yourself any more with the matter, Harris. The matter is quite settled.' Satisfied that the situation had been dealt with as far as it concerned Harris, she turned to make her way back to Miss Sarah's bedside.

'I'm sorry to disagree, ma'am, but I feel it is far from being settled.'

Mrs Oldfield swung back, her face livid. 'How dare you, Harris? You overstep your position time and time again. I will not have it! Do you hear? You deserve to be dismissed!' She swept forwards and snatched the jewellery box out of Ellen's hands. 'Go to bed, before I lose patience with you!'

Ellen moved reluctantly towards the door. She was determined that the matter would not end there! But what could she do?

The door opened from the other side, nearly causing her to overbalance. It was Mr Oldfield. He stepped aside to avoid Ellen. 'Is everything all right, Fay?' he asked his wife. 'I heard raised voices. Is Sarah still unwell?'

Mrs Oldfield recovered her composure. 'She is now sleeping calmly. Harris was just leaving us.'

Ellen knew she must seize this opportunity. She might not get another. 'Miss Sarah's diamond ring has turned up, sir. Isn't that wonderful? Goodnight, sir ... ma'am.'

She slipped through the door and sped along the corridor to the servants' door, leaving Mrs Oldfield to make any explanations to her husband as she thought fit.

Miss Sarah was too ill to rise from her bed the following day. Mrs Oldfield ordered Ellen to attend to any mending that needed to be done and forbade her to make any

169

mention of the ring, either to Miss Sarah, or to anybody else.

It wasn't an easy day. At the best of times, Miss Sarah was well known for her waspish temperament. Suffering from the unaccustomed effects of too much alcohol increased her irritability. Ellen was thankful of the short respites she was given when Mrs Oldfield came to attend to her daughter's needs, allowing Ellen time to eat and refresh herself, but giving her no time to sort out her own mixed emotions.

She sensed that if she weren't in love with Charlie, she would probably now be ready to imagine herself falling in love with John – and that would never do. He was forbidden territory. Even their friendship bordered on lunacy – yet he was the only person with whom she could enjoy a sensible discussion about the things that interested her.

She wondered if he would try to speak with her and was relieved when he didn't. She later heard he had gone motoring with Mr Fairchild.

Monday was washday and, thankfully, Miss Sarah was much recovered, though somewhat pale. After seeing to Miss Sarah's needs and presenting her with a very light breakfast, Ellen was directed to help the downstairs staff. She suspected that Mr and Mrs Oldfield wanted time to talk privately with their daughter.

She was summoned to the library at half past two in the afternoon. Only Mr Oldfield was there. He looked up from his writing.

'Ah, Harris.' He stood up, towering above her, looking extremely uncomfortable. 'The diamond ring, yes? Well, Harris, it appears that Miss Sarah discovered it in one of her purses a few months ago. She didn't know what to do about it and put it away, meaning to confide in her mama and me, but forgot. Very thoughtless, of course but, with her impending engagement and everything, understandable, don't you agree? However, I now feel compelled to make some inquiries to see if Nora can be found and restored back into my household. That will be all. You may go about your duties, Harris.'

Ellen left the room, quietly closing the door, and set off towards the kitchen.

'Psst! Ellen!'

The quiet call of her name made her turn round. It was John. He must have been waiting for her.

'Come in here,' he mouthed silently, nodding towards the dining room door.

She glanced around to make sure no one

else was there before following. 'What's the matter?'

'Nothing. I just wanted to say thank you for being so understanding. I know that Sarah can be a bit difficult at times but she is my sister. I'm sure she sincerely thought the ring had been stolen.'

Ellen nodded. 'Yes, so am I.'

John seemed uneasy ... and so he should! 'Did I embarrass you at the ball? I didn't mean to.' He looked quite penitent but brightened as he added, 'I really did enjoy our dance.'

Ellen smiled wryly. 'I did, too.' What else could she say? It was true; she had enjoyed it.

'I have offended you though, haven't I?'

Ellen hesitated, thinking of the easy friendship that they had always enjoyed. But things were different now. They were no longer children. The way she had felt when he held her in his arms to dance, emphasized that.

'You're the master's son,' she replied at last. 'If your mother even thought that we would talk together like this, she would dismiss me.'

'I'm sorry. I wouldn't want that to happen. You've always been special to me. I can't get used to the way you have suddenly grown up.' He touched her cheek gently with the back of his nails and traced a line along it.

Ellen caught her breath. Didn't he realize what that did to her?

She made a move to go but John held her back by her arm. 'I don't really care what my mother thinks. There are girls at university who are just like you. I can talk with them without upsetting my mother. What's the difference?'

Ellen sighed. 'The difference is they probably come from better families than I do and your mother employs me as your sister's maid. She can sack me whenever she wants, just like Nora was sacked. Then I would be out of a job; homeless and penniless.'

'If you were sacked because of me, I'd make sure you were all right. I wouldn't see you out on the street, even if it made my parents angry with me.'

He was serious, but she shook her head. 'You think it's all so easy, don't you?' She had to laugh at the bewildered, earnest expression on his face. 'You've no idea what it's like to wonder where your next meal is coming from, have you? Or to be so ashamed of the holes in your socks that you don't go to school! Where would I live? Where do you think Nora has been living all this time?' She felt exasperated by his lack of understanding. 'You've no idea what it's like to be poor.'

'Money doesn't matter, Ellen. It's what you are that counts.'

'Yes, I partly agree, but the only ones who say that money doesn't matter are the ones who have plenty of it. Can you imagine what it would be like if your father stopped your allowance? And what would happen when you get married? I can't see a wife taking kindly to her husband "looking after" a former friend, whether a servant or otherwise!'

John looked startled for a moment, then he laughed. 'I'll marry you. That would show my mother! I haven't stopped thinking about you since I kissed you. How about it, Ellen?'

He reached out to touch her hair, but Ellen stepped back, her eyes blazing with anger. 'Stop it! It's not a game. You can't play with people, like this!'

'I'm not playing. I mean it.'

Her anger cooled, as quickly as it had flared. 'You still don't get it, do you?' she said in exasperation. 'It's a totally wrong reason for getting married. You don't love me.'

John was taken aback by her anger. He considered her words. 'I do love you.'

His voice held an element of surprise, as if he'd only just recognized the truth of what he was saying. 'Class doesn't matter. At least, it won't before long. None of the girls at university compares to you; your quickness of mind, your friendly manner, the way we can talk about serious things ... and how lovely you are.' He seized hold of her hands. 'Let's run away and get married before they can stop us. I'm due to return to Cambridge tomorrow. You could come with me. They wouldn't even know until it was too late. What do you say?'

Ellen pulled away again, shaking her head. Her feelings were too mixed up to make a sudden decision like that. 'I can't. I promised I'd wait for Charlie. I'm sure he still loves me.'

His face darkened. 'If he loved you as much as I do, he wouldn't be able to stay away. He'd be right here. But he's not! And I don't think you're indifferent to me!' He put a finger under her chin and lifted her face until her eyes met his. His eyes were warm and loving. He lowered his head and gently touched her lips with his.

A tremor ran through her. She could feel his heart beating and the hardness of his male body, as his hands slipped down to her hips and he pulled her closer. She did have feelings for him ... but was it love, the same kind of love that she felt for Charlie? She wasn't sure. Her body felt aroused by him and the way his mouth moved upon hers made her want to open her lips and invite him in. The most wonderful sensation was spiralling around inside her and she felt an inkling of why Goldie was like she was. But, she wasn't Goldie! And she loved Charlie! And she was only a lady's maid.

John sensed her withdrawal and drew back. 'I really do love you, Ellen. I don't care about our different backgrounds. You know that. Say, yes! Say you'll marry me!'

She moistened her lips. It would be so easy! But, how could she? It wouldn't work. She stepped back, shaking her head. 'No. You would hate me after a while, when the novelty had worn off, when your friends turned away from you, and your family disowned you.'

John's smile faded. 'You don't have a very high opinion of me, do you? You underestimate my feelings for you. I didn't even know it myself, until it came out. But I won't change. I love you, Ellen. I really do!' He picked up her hands again. 'Don't worry,' he said as she flinched, 'I'll leave it for now. I've not been fair to you, springing it on you like this. I'm due home again in a few weeks.

Let's see how we feel about it then, shall we?'

He rested his hands lightly on her shoulders, bent down his head and kissed her gently on the lips but this time without the passion of his previous kiss.

He released her and held open the door, for her to precede him through it. 'Don't forget. I'll be home in June.'

Nine

John returned to Cambridge without further opportunity for them to talk and, if she was honest, she was relieved to see him go. His presence put her emotions in constant turmoil, pulling her one way by her love for the absent Charlie and the other way by her fondness for John.

With a sigh of relief, it seemed, the house settled back into its normal routine, except that they now saw more of Mr Fairchild, heralded by the imperious sound of his klaxon horn. It had been decided that the wedding would be at Christmas, which gave them ample time to make all the necessary plans and preparations. The room next to John's room became known as Mr Fairchild's room and Miss Sarah added fashionable motoring clothes to her wardrobe, delighting in the stir they caused wherever they motored.

June brought in a beautiful summer.

The sun beamed down but Ellen's heart ached as she thought back to the previous summer when Charlie had filled her thoughts, asleep or awake. Not a day went by without her thinking of him. Every clear night she looked up at the stars, looking for their own bright star. Whatever the reason for Charlie not writing to her, she knew he hadn't forgotten her. He couldn't have. She'd know. They had promised ... both of them. They had made plans; built their dreams. Was that all it was, a dream? Did his few letters convey the real hopes of his heart? How could they, when there were so many weeks between each one? She knew he was busy; that he worked hard. But so did she; yet she could still find time to write. If he loved her, he would too!

How it hurt! Especially when she allowed the thought that he had stopped loving her to take hold. She had heard of people dying of a broken heart, but that was only in stories, surely. Now, she felt it could be possible to actually die of heartbreak!

She busied herself in her work; outings to town with Miss Sarah; trips to the dressmakers and milliners; tea parties; dinner parties; motor outings. She knew she was fortunate. Her duties were pleasant but somewhat tedious. She would rather be using her mind than her nimble fingers, which had somehow learned how to stitch in a piece of the finest lace or mend a tear in the hem of one of Miss Sarah's gowns so that not even the most pernickety of mistresses would notice.

The emptiness in her heart over Charlie's seeming desertion found no ease. She'd loved him. She still did so ... why did he not write?

And Mr Fairchild was getting bolder, too. Pinching her bottom when she passed by, running his hand along her arm or even across her cheek. She tried to make sure she was never alone with him but it wasn't always possible.

One morning, she was serving at the breakfast table. Mr Oldfield had a rather quick breakfast, far quicker than Mrs Oldfield would have allowed him to eat if she had been present. But she and Miss Sarah were having breakfast in their rooms after an exciting motor ride to Chester the previous day.

'I have a special journey to make today,' Mr Oldfield commented to Mr Fairchild, who had stayed overnight. He turned round to face Ellen. 'I would be obliged if you would remind Mrs Garland to be flexible over the timing for dinner this evening, Harris. I may be a little late. I'm sorry to be deserting you, Leslie. Cadman is coming with me but Harris will make sure you have all you need.'

Ellen kept all expression from her face. Not if she could help it, she wouldn't!

After Mr Oldfield had departed, Ellen stood stiffly at the serving station, refusing to glance over to where Mr Fairchild was seated. He had eaten well, partaking of devilled kidneys, slices of bacon, poached eggs, grilled tomatoes and mushrooms. Now that he was alone, he lingered over the remainder of his breakfast.

'Pass the toast, m'dear.' He leaned back in his chair, watching closely as she stepped forwards to place the toast rack near to his left hand. He waited until she had stepped back again. 'And the butter.' It was nearer to him than it was to her but she quietly walked past him, to the other side of the table and pushed it nearer.

'What's the matter, Harris? I know what you are after. I can read it in your eyes.

Come on. I won't tell anyone.' He patted his outstretched legs. 'Come and sit here, on Uncle Leslie's lap. You can feed me some toast. Pretend that I'm Mamma's little boy. You'd like that, wouldn't you?'

Ellen was revolted. Was he joking? Did he expect her to laugh with him? Her eyes flickered towards the door, praying that it would open and someone would come in.

Keeping his eyes upon her, Mr Fairchild pushed back his chair and stood up. He carefully wiped his lips with the edge of his napkin and dropped it onto his abandoned side plate. 'Now, don't be going coy on me, Harris. Not after all those fluttering eyes that you've made at me.'

Ellen felt a flurry of alarm. 'Don't come any nearer,' she warned, as he moved towards her. 'I warn you, I shall scream.' Wanting something in her hands between them, she grabbed hold of the coffee pot as she backed away.

Mr Fairchild smiled. 'There's no one to hear you, m'dear. And why scream, when you know you want it as much as I do? I can give a girl like you a good time and make it worth your while. You'll come back for more, like Goldie does. Ask her what she thinks of me. She can't get enough.'

'Well, I'm not Goldie!' she snapped at him. 'So, leave me alone!' She swung on her heels and made for the door.

Mr Fairchild strode forward and reached the door as she did. He grabbed hold of her and pushed her, face forward, against the door. 'I like a girl with spirit. We'll play it that way, if that's what you want,' he murmured in her ear. He twisted her round, immediately covered her mouth with his own, thrusting his tongue between her teeth. She felt as though she was choking. All the revulsion and terror she had known as a child flooded back into her mind. The smell of him sickened her and the touch of his moustache on her face, the slobbering of his mouth, filled her with loathing.

The coffee pot was still in her hand. She curled her fingers tightly round the handle and swung it with all the strength she could muster against Fairchild's back. It wasn't a hard blow, but it was enough. The hot coffee spilled from the spout against his neck. He swore savagely as he reeled sideways.

Ellen sprang free and yanked the door open.

'Bitch! You'll be sorry for this!' Fairchild snarled at her, his hand to his neck.

Ellen didn't linger. She fled along the hall

to the servants' door and down to the kitchen, bursting abruptly through the doorway. Feeling weak with shock, she leaned back against the door. How dare he? The loathsome, disgusting animal! Her lips involuntarily drew back, as the revulsion she felt rose from her stomach and threatened to erupt from her mouth.

'Ellen! Whatever's the matter?' cried Mrs Garland, dropping the pan that she was lifting down from a shelf. The other maids gaped at her.

Mrs Garland was already crossing the kitchen, pulling a wooden chair with her as she went. 'Sit yourself down on this, Ellen. Wet that cloth, Patty, and bring it over here. Pour a cup of tea, Doris, and put a good spoonful of sugar in it. Now, take some deep breaths, Ellen. Don't try to talk yet. Let's get you fit, first.' Mrs Garland's round face was full of concern.

Ellen's throat was still tight and dry. 'It was Mr Fairchild. He grabbed hold of me. He ... he...' She couldn't say it. Her voice shook. 'It was horrible.'

Goldie gave a nervous laugh. 'I bet you led him on. He's always saying how you make eyes at him.'

Ellen rounded on her. 'No, I don't. I've

183

never led him on. I do my best to keep out of his way. Not like you. He said how much you enjoy his attentions!'

'I only flirt with him,' Goldie said quickly, with a sidelong look at Mrs Garland. 'He only wants a bit of slap and tickle. It's easier to play along with him. It keeps him happy.'

'You'd better be careful, Goldie!' Mrs Garland warned. 'We've all heard tales of what happens in some establishments when the menfolk get too familiar with the servants. And it's not all just tales. I don't want none of it in my establishment.'

Goldie tossed her head. 'I can look after myself. I know how far to go and still keep him happy. Ellen could do with a bit of excitement in her life.'

'That's enough, Goldie! Get back to work,' Mrs Garland ordered. 'As for you, Ellen, try to keep out of his way as much as you can. It's a bit awkward, you being Miss Sarah's maid and all that. I don't suppose you'd like to see if the missus will do a swap with you and Goldie?'

Goldie laughed. 'Not likely! I wouldn't last a day with Miss Sarah!'

Cook spread her hands. 'That's true. You'll just have to keep a sharp look out for him, Ellen.'

Ellen nodded. 'I always do.'

The rest of the servants got on with their various tasks, Goldie taking a light lunch up to the dining room for the two ladies and their guest. Dinner was prepared but kept on hold as Mrs Oldfield waited for her husband's return.

As the usual time for dinner came and went, Mrs Garland was bobbing around the kitchen like an anxious hen.

'Pull those vegetables off the heat, Agnes, or they'll be overcooked. And keep an eye on that sauce, Doris. I don't want it burning and to have to be done all over again.'

As she spoke, everyone became aware that the inner door at the top of the steps had opened and a hesitant figure began to descend. Her clothes were poor and not as clean as they might have been. Her hair was lank, framing a thin face. Her eyes showed apprehension, as they flickered from one to another of the faces upturned towards her, none registering recognition. Her lips formed a hesitant smile.

Mrs Garland was the first to react.

'Nora! It's Nora!' she cried, rushing forwards with outstretched arms, enveloping the young woman in her embrace. 'Oh,

185

Nora, you've come back!'

Dinner was almost thrown onto the table and, at the insistence of the master, only Cadman remained upstairs to attend to their employers' needs. Everyone else rushed through the necessary jobs in the kitchen, whilst Nora sat in the rocking chair by the range, her hands around a cup of tea, her eyes taking in the once familiar surroundings. Every so often, tears flowed unchecked down her cheeks, as past memories and recent deprivations met together.

'I couldn't believe it when I realized that it was Mr Oldfield,' she said, more than once. 'He came to find me! He said it was all a mistake and the ring had been found. He said Ellen found it.' She turned towards Ellen and reached out a hand to her.

'Aye, and she's a dark horse, our Ellen. Never a word of it to any of us,' Mrs Garland exclaimed, half scolding.

'Mr Oldfield asked me not to say anything until he had found Nora. He didn't want to raise our hopes, in case it came to nothing.'

'Or unless Mrs Oldfield put a stop to it, more likely,' Goldie suggested, adding slyly, 'Of course, we know that Ellen has the ear of them upstairs, especially their guests!'

'Stop it, Goldie. You're only jealous of her,'

Doris flashed at her with a rare burst of spirit.

Nora waved her hand to stop the arguing. 'I can't believe how grown up you all are.' Tears flowed again, followed by a few more sips of her tea.

'Put the kettle back on, Agnes,' Mrs Garland ordered. 'Bert'll be down soon. And have some of this semolina, Nora. You need your strength building up again.'

'I'll soon do that, now I'm back here.' Nora smiled through her tears. 'I thought about you all so often. I can tell you this, we might grumble about our life here but compared to some other places, this here place is like heaven.'

Over the next few hours, they learned most of what had befallen Nora after her dismissal. It didn't make pleasant hearing. She told them of days of wandering the streets; getting a lift to Blackburn and then to Preston; being reduced to stealing food from market stalls; and being sent to the workhouse as a vagrant.

She shuddered at the memory of it. 'It was awful. The smells, the noise, the dirt and the squalor. I thought I'd go mad in there. I can't remember how long I was there, only that it was like your worst nightmares. We used to get casual seasonal work on farms and then I got took on as a maid on one of the farms. And that were no picnic, I can tell you. At the mistress's beck and call all day long, I was ... and looking after three unruly children. Then, just before Christmas, the master began to pester me and when I told the mistress, she said I'd lured him on and she sacked me. She just threw me out ... and I was back in the workhouse. And that's where Mr Oldfield found me. Oh, it's good to be back.'

It was so lovely to have Nora back with them that no one thought of any repercussions to the rest of the staff. However, a week later, Mrs Garland entered the kitchen from her weekly meeting with Mrs Oldfield in the parlour with an anxious expression on her face.

'Goldie, can I see you for a minute?' she asked, as Goldie appeared in the kitchen with her arms full of mats from upstairs.

'Now?'

'Yes, please. Come into the storeroom with me.'

Goldie put the mats by the kitchen door and followed Mrs Garland, wondering what it was about. 'What's up?' she asked, looking slightly defiant. 'What've I done?'

'Nothing. For once, it's nothing you've done.' Mrs Garland looked uncomfortable.

'What is it, then? You're obviously going to tell me something I don't want to hear.'

'Mrs Oldfield has decided that Nora can have her old position back now she knows that she didn't steal the ring.'

Goldie's face fell. 'What about me? Am I getting the sack?'

'Nay, though we've to lose Agnes. You can become chief parlourmaid and help down here when we need you.'

Goldie's face flared. 'In other words, I'm a "tweeny" again! Well, she can keep it!'

'Now, don't speak first and then think about it afterwards,' Mrs Garland cautioned. 'She won't drop your money. Not yet, anyway.'

'Why me?' Goldie demanded. 'Why not Ellen? I've been here longer than she has.'

'I know. But you said yourself you'd never manage as Miss Sarah's maid. You'd be on your way in less than no time!'

'Well, it's not fair! I bet they're all laughing at me, aren't they?'

'I haven't told them yet. I wanted to tell you first, so as you'll be prepared. You could pretend you'll like it. It won't be so bad. You've done it before.'

'It's Ellen's fault. Why couldn't she leave things as they were? Right smug, she is, taking the credit for getting Nora back. She should learn to mind her own business.'

'Now, now. You know you don't mean that,' Mrs Garland cajoled. 'You wouldn't have wanted Nora to be left where she was, would you? Come on. We'll tell the others. Get a smile on your face.'

To Goldie's credit, she did just that – but she determined to get even.

Entering the kitchen a few days later to make a cup of tea for Miss Sarah, Ellen was surprised to see Goldie leap up from the fireside seat, thrusting her hands behind her back. A flush rose up her cheeks.

'What're you up to?' Ellen asked. 'You're obviously doing something you shouldn't.'

'It's none of your business,' Goldie retorted. 'I thought you were Cook coming in, that's all. I didn't want her to find me sitting down. You know what she's like.'

She turned her back on Ellen and tossed some pieces of paper into the fire, pushing them down into the flames with the poker.

Shrugging slightly, Ellen began to prepare the tea tray. Miss Sarah and her mother were being driven to Bolton later, when Mr Fairchild had made his appearance. Now that it had been decided that the wedding was to be a few days before Christmas, they were calling at Beckett's, the printer's in Horwich, to discuss the necessary stationery requirements and then going to Whitaker's in Bolton to look at fabrics for Miss Sarah's wedding gown.

Goldie continued the taunt. 'No letter again, Ellen, I noticed. I think he's forgotten about you ... but then, he hadn't much to remember, had he?'

'He's busy,' Ellen said, defending Charlie. 'He has a lot to do.'

'I bet he has! Not on his own, either, I'd say! I wonder how many girls he's had since he went down there. How long has it been? Nearly a year now, isn't it? A lot can happen in a year. He could be married – or have got a more obliging girl than you pregnant.'

Ellen flushed. She knew Goldie was deliberately goading her. Any signs of friendship that had built up over the years had recently faded, though she couldn't think why, unless it was because she was still Miss Sarah's maid and Goldie now a 'tweeny' again – though that wasn't her fault.

The following day, Ellen was in the kitchen when the postman arrived. She didn't often see him, as she was usually still attending to Miss Sarah at this time of the morning.

The postman dropped his sack at the door and put his bundle of letters of letters down on the kitchen table.

Ellen saw that her name was on the top letter. Her heart leapt. A letter from Charlie!

'Oh, so you're the lucky lady, are you?' the postman teased. 'You keep me in a job, you do, miss.' He reached over and slid the letter out from the string that held the bundle together.

Once it was in her hand, the eager light faded from her eyes. She could tell it wasn't from Charlie. It wasn't his handwriting, though it did seem familiar. She slipped it into the front of her apron to read later, when she was on her own.

Goldie looked uneasy. As soon as the post-man had gone and Cook had left the kitchen, she started to probe. 'Who's your letter off, then? Aren't you going to read it?'

'I'll read it later, when your nosy eyes aren't on it.'

'Ooh! It's like that, is it? Come on, let's all have a read.' Goldie darted her hand inside Ellen's apron bib and pulled the letter out, waving it high in the air.

'Give it back, Goldie. You've no right to do

that.' Ellen tried to reach the letter but Goldie ran round the kitchen table and climbed up onto a chair, still holding the letter high aloft.

'Well, it's not from Charlie,' she declared. 'You must have another admirer. Ooh, I wonder who it is. Let's see, shall we?' She looked around quickly, making sure Mrs Garland was still out of the way, and tore open the envelope.

Ellen tried to snatch it back but Goldie kept turning round to keep the letter out of reach. As she began to read, her eyes widened in surprise. 'No wonder you didn't want an audience, you dark horse! You have been setting your sights high! And here we were, thinking you were still missing Charlie! Listen to this, everyone.

My dearest Ellen,

Are you missing me like I am missing you? I can still taste the sweetness of your lips, from that stolen kiss. I long to see you again but I am begging you to release me from the promise to come home in June. My good friend, Edward Cholmondeley (Goldie pronounced each syllable), has invited me to accompany him on a tour of Europe. Please understand, I can't let an opportunity like this pass by. It's the chance of a lifetime. I will think of you every day. Don't forget me. I'll be home at the end of August. I keep you in my heart. With undying love, from...'

Goldie paused dramatically, enjoying the spectacle of the upturned faces, their eyes fixed on her. Her own eyes were alight with mischievous delight. Wow, was she going to shock them all! Just wait till they heard! She could read the apprehension in Ellen's eyes. Well, this would show her up for what she was, little miss goody!

Ten

Mrs Garland had re-entered the kitchen and was about to order Goldie to come down off the chair, when Goldie continued to drop her bombshell.

'...with undying love, from ... John.'

The kitchen fell silent and Ellen felt her face grow hot. What was John thinking of? Did he never think of the consequences of his actions?

194

'Now, who do we know called John?' Goldie asked, hands on her hips. 'It wouldn't be Mr John, the master's son, would it?'

All eyes turned to look at Ellen.

'I ... d-don't know why he's written that,' she stammered. 'It's a joke. He was teasing me the last time he was home.'

'It's a joke, all right,' Goldie agreed. 'Just think what Mrs Oldfield will say! It'll be no joke then – except to the rest of us. I hope we all get to see it!'

Mrs Garland broke into the stunned silence. 'Give over, Goldie, and get down off that chair.'

Goldie reluctantly obeyed. Not one to give in easily, she waggled the letter in Ellen's face. 'You've really done it this time,' she chortled.

Ellen grabbed at the letter, tearing most of it out of Goldie's grasp. 'You've no right to read my letters,' she protested angrily. 'Don't ever do that again!'

'Ooh! Getting tough, are we? And what are you going to do about it?'

'Goldie! I've told you to give up,' Mrs Garland intervened again. 'Now, put the rest of that letter down and go and get on with your work.'

Goldie slammed the scraps of paper onto

the kitchen table and flounced out of the kitchen, with a backward look of triumph at Ellen. The other kitchen staff returned to their tasks, leaving her to face Mrs Garland.

Mrs Garland sighed with exasperation. 'I don't know what you've been up to, Ellen, but I can tell you this. You're playing with fire. Joke or not, that letter could spell dismissal for you.' She jerked her head towards the kitchen door. 'You can't count on Goldie not saying anything. A little word from her and Mrs Oldfield will be down on you like a ton of bricks. You'll be out of that door quicker than your feet can take you. And as for Mr John, he should know better.' She shook her head impatiently. 'You'd better burn that letter and hope that Goldie doesn't say anything. And be warned, them upstairs never marry the likes of us, whatever your romantic stories might say.'

Ellen felt indignant. 'We're just good friends. At least–' She remembered John's kisses. 'Anyway, we've haven't done anything wrong. We enjoy talking together. We discuss books and politics and–'

'Aye, and Mr John comes home and finds that you've suddenly grown up. He's naïve if he thinks he can marry you. His mother would never allow it; nor his father. In fact, I wouldn't be surprised to learn that Mrs Oldfield was behind that invitation to tour Europe. She's seen the way he looks at you, like the rest of us have. If you went away with him, married or not, it would ruin him.'

Ellen thought of John's last words to her after Miss Sarah's ring had been found and, yes, he did cause a spark of excitement in her heart. Her thoughts flew to him more and more these days, especially when Charlie's letters didn't come. Had he been serious? She knew he thought he was but he hadn't contacted her until now.

She raised her eyes to meet Mrs Garland's. 'Perhaps you're right. I didn't really take him seriously. I told him so. It was the thrill of the ring being found.'

'Well, the thrill's over, as far as you're concerned. You're stuck with the reality. As I said before, burn the letter and keep your head down.'

It was a hot August. The kitchen range had to be lit whatever the weather, though, and it was almost unbearable in there, even when the door and windows were wide open – as they were from dawn until dusk. Even the upstairs rooms, that Ellen now frequented more than downstairs, were incredibly stuffy.

The house had been designed to withstand the cold winters more than allow for a hot summer.

Ellen spent most of her afternoons off cycling along the country lanes around Rivington and Anglezarke and, sometimes, out towards Bolton. She loved the freedom that her bicycle gave her. She had been into the ladies' clothing department in the large Co-operative store on Lee Lane on the pretext of being there on behalf of her mistress and had examined some of the new divided skirts that some bolder young ladies were wearing. Thankful that she had watched her grandma, as she had cut out and sewn some of her frocks, she had laboriously altered one of Miss Sarah's cast-offs into such a garment for herself; it didn't matter that the seams at the top of the divide weren't quite as neatly done as the shop-bought garments.

The good weather continued. Most of the farmers were busy hay-making. She wondered if Charlie would come home to help on the family farms and, if he did, would he find a way to come to see her? The last Tuesday of the month dawned brightly. Ellen rushed through her work so that it was all done before lunch. It was a perfect day for cycling. The sun gently caressed her cheeks, highlighting her freckles. She didn't care. A slight breeze cooled down the temperature and made the narrow lanes, bordered with rich hedgerows, idyllic surroundings.

She headed along Chorley Old Road towards Bolton, secretly hoping she might somehow pass one of the Metcalfe farms and recognize either of the two of Charlie's brothers she had met briefly the previous year.

It didn't happen. The farm workers she saw struck no chord of memory and she didn't feel bold enough to call at any of the farms to ask if they knew of Charlie and his whereabouts. How foolish she would feel if Goldie's taunts were true and he had married someone else.

Feeling lower in spirit than when she had set out, she headed for home. She had just turned into Chapel Lane when she became aware that a motor car was behind her, though the driver made no move to overtake her. She cast a glance over her shoulder and realized with dismay that it was Mr Fairchild.

Why didn't he pass her? She felt a light bump against her rear mudguard. It took all of her skill to keep upright. What was he playing at?

His front bumper touched again ... and

again. Then, as they were approaching a right-hand bend, bordered by a high grass verge, the motor car drew level with her. With a stab of alarm, she realized that he was forcing her into the grassy bank at her left-hand side. Her pedal dug into the soft earth and grass, bringing her bicycle to an abrupt halt and flinging her over the handlebars and onto the verge. Her divided skirt caught on the metal framework, pulling the bicycle on top of her.

With a triumphant 'toot-toot' of the horn, the car sped away. Ellen fell back against the grass verge, eyes closed for a moment as she caught her breath. Relief that she wasn't hurt turned to anger. How dare he?

Her fury gave strength to her limbs and she managed to sit up and disentangle herself from the frame of her bicycle. As she scrambled to her feet, the sound of another motorized vehicle made her listen intently. Was Mr Fairchild returning to taunt her further?

With a sense of relief, she realized the sound was coming from her right, from Chorley Old Road, and a motorized hackney cab came into view. The driver was slowing down, speaking over his shoulder to his passenger. As the passenger pushed his head out of the window, both he and Ellen gave a cry of recognition. It was John. He was home!

He leaped from the cab, even before it had fully stopped, and ran towards her. She was so relieved to see him that she dropped hold of her bicycle, ran straight into his arms and burst into tears.

'Ellen! What's happened? Are you all right?' He held her against him, stroking her hair, easing her distress.

She tried to pull herself together, despising herself for crying. 'I'm sorry; I'm being foolish. I was all right until I saw you!'

John laughed. 'Well, I don't know whether that's a compliment or not! I've been thinking about you all summer, wondering if you were missing me, but I didn't expect such a ready welcome. Have you missed me? Did you get the letter that I sent you?'

A shadow flickered across her face.

'Yes, I did!'

In some measure of indignation, she told him of the trouble it had caused, glad, for the moment to take the spotlight off herself.

John was immediately contrite. 'I'm sorry. I didn't think anyone else would see it.' He traced his finger down the left side of her cheek.

Ellen felt her heart skip a beat. It felt so good to be held so close but she knew she shouldn't be letting him do this. She drew away, raising her face to answer his question. As their eyes locked, the words remained unspoken. Before either had time to give any thought, their lips were touching, each responding to the other.

Ellen recalled Cook saying that any liaison between them would ruin him – and she pulled away. 'No, we mustn't.'

'I'm sorry. You're right. This isn't the right place,' John apologized, misinterpreting her motive in moving away from him. 'So, tell me what's happened here. What made you fall off your bicycle?'

She shook back her hair, taking the opportunity to wipe the back of her fingers against her eyes. 'It was Mr Fairchild! He ran me off the road! He needn't think that I won't complain! He's gone too far this time!'

She turned away, to pick up her bicycle.

'Who?'

'Mr Fairchild! Who else? No one else is capable of it!'

John looked appalled. 'Leslie? Sarah's Leslie? You must be mistaken. He wouldn't do that to you!'

'Wouldn't he just? He was playing with

me, like a cat plays with a mouse; then, he edged his car right into me and ran me into the bank. I couldn't avoid it.'

'Maybe he cut the corner too finely. He probably isn't as good a driver as he makes out.'

She shook her head. 'It wasn't like that. He did it deliberately. And it's not all he does! He's forever at me, pinching my bottom, grabbing hold of me and trying to get me to kiss him – or worse! It's disgusting and I hate him!'

John looked troubled. 'I'm sure you must be mistaken. He's besotted with Sarah. You must have got it wrong.'

Ellen jerked her bicycle upright and set it down between them. 'I'm not mistaken. It's true. I daren't be alone with him but I don't expect you to believe me; I'm only a servant.'

She made to move away with her bicycle but John grasped hold of the handlebars. 'You know I don't think like that – but you're making serious allegations. It would break Sarah's heart.' He paused and reached out to touch her hair again. 'You said yourself he was playing with you. You're a very pretty girl. He's probably just being friendly.'

Ellen's spirit flagged. It was a waste of

time trying to explain. 'Forget it. It doesn't concern you.'

John felt hurt. 'If it concerns you, I'll make it concern me,' he promised. 'I've missed you so much while I've been away, wondering if I made the wrong decision to go to Europe.' He reached out towards her, trying to take hold of her again but she stepped away.

'No. Please; we mustn't.'

'Why not? I've waited all summer for this moment. You can't let whatever you think Leslie tried to do come between us. I love you. And don't pretend you don't care for me because I know that you do.'

Ellen raised her eyes and studied his face for a moment. His expression was full of concern for her but she shook her head. Cook was right; she was playing with fire – and they would both get burned. She couldn't do that to him.

She hardened her voice. 'We live worlds apart, John. And I still love Charlie.'

Disappointment flitted across John's face. 'Has he been in touch with you?'

'No.' Her voice was no more than a whisper.

'Then, how do you know he still cares for you? He might have another girl by now.'

His bluntness hurt; he could be right. 'I

don't know. I just don't know, John! Can't you see? I just can't make any decisions until I know!'

'He doesn't deserve you.' John's voice was gruff with emotion. 'He should have taken you with him. I would. I could take you with me now. I don't mind if you don't love me as much as I love you. I'll take that chance. I know it would work out all right. I get quite a good allowance. Mother and Father needn't know. We could keep it a secret until I've finished at university.'

She shook her head. 'I couldn't live like that. I want my man to be proud of me, not ashamed of me, having to hide me away.'

'I'm not ashamed of you,' he protested. 'It's just that Mother wouldn't understand. They would stop my allowance.'

'If you really loved me, that wouldn't stop you displeasing your parents.' She knew she sounded peevish, which wasn't fair of her, really. She was the one putting objections in the way. But she couldn't think straight. What should she do?

'I do love you and I want you so badly. Come away with me, Ellen! We could go right now. They don't know I'm due home today. I could just write and ask them to send my trunk to Cambridge. They wouldn't know until it was too late!'

Ellen's heart lurched within her. She was tempted. She didn't doubt he believed he loved her. But Cook's words rang in her head. 'They never marry the likes of us. They want you on their terms.' And even if he did marry her, it would ruin his life. She mustn't encourage him. She'd have to find another way to get away from Mr Fairchild.

'I'm sorry, John.' She looked away and bit her lip. 'I do have feelings for you but I still love Charlie. I must wait for him.'

John silently searched her face. He saw the uncertainty. Anger against Charlie burned in his heart. 'He has no right to treat you like this! You deserve better! I'll wait for you until I know that there's no more hope for me – and that will only be when Charlie makes you his wife, if he ever comes back for you, or when you can look me in the face when you say that you don't love me.'

In heavy silence, he fixed her bicycle on the back of the cab and they climbed inside. When they approached the front gates, it was Ellen who leaned forward and spoke to the driver. 'Stop here, please.'

John lifted down her bicycle and she wheeled it round to the back entrance, leaving John to enter by the front door.

Their encounter on the roadside raised a barrier between them that neither knew how to overcome for the moment. Ellen didn't want to risk being tempted to allow herself to be charmed by his talk of loving her. John seemed to be protecting his hurt emotions by treating her with almost the same cool disdain as his mother did.

Before either knew of it, it was time for John to return to Cambridge.

She didn't mention the incident of her cycle ride to Cook. Neither did she complain to Miss Sarah about Mr Fairchild's behaviour. She wasn't fully sure why she didn't. Maybe it was because she didn't expect to be believed – or was it because, as John had said, it would devastate his sister? Whatever her reason, she kept silent and tried to keep her distance from Mr Fairchild, hoping he would tire of his game.

Winter set in early with a vengeance, that year. The North West was battered by storms.

A raw November swept in. Even indoors it was difficult to keep warm. The wind found its way through every crack in the window frames and through every gap in the rafters.

Outdoor work was done hurriedly. No one

felt like lingering at the front of the house whilst whitening the steps or polishing the brass door-fittings. They scurried back to the warmth of the kitchen or lingered near the fires in the upper rooms whilst they were there to do the dusting and polishing.

Goldie looked pale and shivery.

'Whatever's the matter with you?' Cook demanded. 'You've done nothing but keep slipping out all morning. Have you got a fella out there?'

Goldie shook her head, not even rising to the bait. 'I'm all right. I just need a bit of fresh air.'

'Well, there's plenty of that out there. Here, go and peg these clothes out, while you're at it. I may as well make use of your flitting in and out.'

The cold day drew on. A few snowflakes were seen to twirl through the air and land on the ground but it was too wet to stick. By evening, everyone felt cold through to their bones.

'Can't you get any nearer to that fire?' Cook asked sarcastically, looking at everyone crowding round the warmest place in the kitchen. 'I hope you filled the upstairs coal scuttles to the tops, Patty, or you'll be having to go out for some more.' She lifted the corner of the dark woven cloth that draped over the sides of the wooden table by the door. 'The spare buckets under here need filling, so you'd better do them now.'

'Aw! It's cold! And I don't like it out there in the dark, Cook,' Patty protested. 'Someone might jump on me!'

Goldie managed a weak grin. 'You should be so lucky! Go on. Get out there. This might be your big moment.'

'Will you come with me?' Patty asked.

'Not likely. I've had enough big moments, thank you. I'm not moving from this fireside until it's time to go to bed.'

'Aw, go on.' Patty looked round at her huddled friends.

'I'll come with you,' Ellen offered. She picked up the bucket from the fireside. 'Get your shawl fastened round your shoulders and fetch the other buckets.'

They forced their way outside against the wind and Cook banged the door shut behind them. 'Knock loud, when you want to come back in,' she shouted.

A door creaked and banged, rocking on its hinges. Patty grabbed hold of Ellen's arm. 'I don't like it out here. There's shadows all over.'

'Shut up, Patty! You'll waken the dead!'

Ellen shouted in exasperation. 'Look. I'll fill one of your buckets first, then you can go back in.' She quickly piled coal into one of Patty's buckets then said, 'Go on; and don't drop any!'

Patty thankfully trudged back to the kitchen door. It opened at her shout and was banged shut again. Ellen shovelled at the coal pile as quickly as she could, not quite as nonchalant as she had made out. She suddenly stopped and listened. 'What was that?'

There was only the sound of the wind and the various doors creaking and banging. She'd best pull herself together before she got the jitters as well.

The sound came again. It was like a cough, hastily cut off. To satisfy her peace of mind, she went over to the woodshed doorway. The door had been blown half off its hinges and rattled against the wall. Inside, it was pitch black. She stood in the doorway. All was quiet but, as she turned to go, another muffled cough stopped her.

'Who's there?' she shouted, more bravely than she felt. 'I can hear you. Come on out or I'll go for help.'

There was a sharp gasp, then silence.

'You may as well come out,' she tried again. 'If you don't, I'll go and get some of

210

the men to come out,' crossing her fingers, since there was only Bert.

She turned, to do as she had threatened, but a trembling voice stopped her. 'Is that you, our Ellen?'

'What?' The use of her name startled her. 'Who are you? Come on out!'

'It's me – Tom!' There was a scrambling noise and the sound of falling wood.

Ellen peered into the darkness. 'Tom? I don't believe it! What on earth are you doing here? Come on out! I can't see you in there.'

With a slithering and falling of wood, Tom struggled out of his hiding place. He was much taller than she remembered but, even in the gloom, it was unmistakably him! She flung her arms around him. 'Tom! It really is you! Oh, it's so good to see you! How you've grown! You're nearly as big as me. But what are you doing here?'

Tom wiped his sleeve across his face. 'I had to come, Ellen. I couldn't stand it no more. Our stepdad kept beating me and kicking me. I didn't dare be in the house with him, especially when he's been drinking ... and that's nearly all the time.'

'Oh, Tom!' She hugged him again, wondering if she would wake up and find out she'd been dreaming.

'I ran off to our grandma's.' He was shivering violently.

'Let's get you back inside the woodshed, out of this cold wind,' Ellen interrupted him, shivering nearly as much as Tom. She sat down on a pile of logs and drew her brother into her arms to try to warm up his thin body. She put her shawl round his shoulders. 'Go on,' she encouraged him. 'What happened next?'

'I stayed a few days with Grandma but I was afraid Zach would come after me. Grandma told me how to find you and gave me a bit of money but I spent some of it on something to eat. Then, when I managed to find me way to t'railway station, I hadn't enough for a ticket. I hung outside for a while and, when I got the chance, I went in with a group of people. Nob'dy took any notice of me, so I found out where the train to Bolton went from and I sneaked on board. I hid under a seat. It was a bit scary at times.

'I must have fallen asleep, 'cos all of a sudden, it was quiet. Well, there was shouting and banging of doors but I could tell that the train had stopped and the carriage was empty. I crawled out to see where we were and this guard saw me! I was scared stiff. He threw me off t'train said I'd no right to be in t'station. He thought I'd just got on!'

He laughed at the memory of it. 'An engine driver was just going by. He asked if I liked trains. I said yes and he said I could go and have a look at the engine. I told him I was trying to find you and he said his train was coming here and, if I promised never to tell, I could ride in his cab! It was great! Then I found out where Mr Oldfield's house was and came here. I thought if I could find you, you might be able to get me a job and somewhere to stay.'

A shout, above the sound of the wind, broke into Tom's account. 'Ellen! Are you coming in? What're you doing out there?'

Ellen leapt to the door and waved the shovel in the direction of where Mrs Garland was framed in the kitchen doorway.

What could she do? If she took Tom inside, someone might tell Mrs Oldfield; she'd never let him stay. She turned quickly back to Tom.

'I've got to go back in. I'll just take one bucket, then I can come back out for the other one. I'll see if there's anything I can pick up for you to eat.'

She picked up one of the buckets of coal and quickly crossed the yard with it. Her mind was racing. Whatever could she do with him? He had a bad cough. He shouldn't be left outside. Ooh! Their stepfather had a lot to answer for!

Mrs Garland opened the door for her. 'Whatever have you been doing out there, Ellen? Digging for the coal yourself, were you? And where's your shawl and the other bucket?'

'My shawl blew off; and I couldn't carry both buckets, Cook. I filled it too full,' marvelling at the ready lies upon her lips. 'I'll go back for it.' She put the bucket down, inside the doorway. She could see that Goldie was toasting some bread. 'That looks good, Goldie. Can I have a piece before I go back for the other bucket?'

'Toast your own. I'm not your slave!'

'Right! Then you can get out for the coal!' Cook snapped. 'Ellen was the only one who offered to help Patty. You've done nothing but mope about for weeks! At the very least, you could give her a piece of toast!'

'It's all right...' Ellen began. She couldn't have Goldie going out there.

Just in time, Goldie tossed a piece of toast to her. 'You can put your own butter on it!'

'What, with hands that colour? You'll poison yourself!' Cook objected. 'Here, Patty. You do it.'

Patty slapped a layer of butter onto the toast and handed it to Ellen.

'Now get that down you, before you go back outside,' Cook suggested.

'I'll eat it as I go, Cook. I'll be quicker back in then.'

'Well, don't go down the mine for it, this time,' Cook retorted, 'or I'll be locking the door on you!'

Ellen escaped back outside and ran across to the woodshed. 'Tom! It's me! Come and get this toast. I daren't stay. I'll be back later, I promise.'

Tom grabbed the toast and pushed it at his mouth.

'Thanks, Ellen. It's lovely. Go on. I'll be all right.'

'I'll bar the door to keep the wind out. See you later!'

She hated leaving him. There were still lots of questions to ask him. It was ages since she had heard from her mam. She hoped she was all right; and the little ones. Not that they would be all that little now, she reflected.

She quickly made plans as she struggled back across the yard with the heavy coal bucket. She'd have to wait until Goldie had gone to sleep; then she could creep downstairs and fetch Tom into the warm kitchen. There might be something she could find to wrap around him when he had to go back out again. Their Tom hadn't half landed her in a pickle – but it was grand to see him again.

It was a while before the family had settled down for the night and the servants were free to make their own way upstairs. Miss Sarah found fault with everything that Ellen did for her; her hands were too cold; she preferred the other nightgown; the brush pulled at her hair; the fire was too smoky. But, at long last, she was settled and Ellen bade her goodnight.

Goldie was already in bed and dopey with sleep as Ellen crept into bed with her clothes on and lay as still as she could, waiting for the regular breathing to tell her that Goldie was fast asleep. It was hard to keep awake but she didn't dare drop off or she would sleep until morning. The creaking of the stairs told her that Nora was coming upstairs to her tiny room and, later, she heard the heavy tread of Cook's footsteps. She was always the last to leave the kitchen, so Ellen knew that Bert would have also retired for the night.

She lay very still and counted to a hundred. Then she quietly slid off the bed, inwardly groaning at the twang of the springs. Goldie stirred and turned over. Ellen froze, waiting until Goldie's breathing settled down again. She tiptoed to the door, willing it not to creak as she opened it.

All was quiet in the kitchen. There was still a small glow from the fire, enough to enable her to see her way. She put a few pieces of coal on it and put an extra brick to warm, before she went to unbar the large kitchen door.

It was still very cold and windy. The wind whipped up her skirt as she ran across the yard to the woodshed. Her hair flew wildly about her face as she tugged at the bar on the woodshed door. The door opened suddenly, almost flinging her off her feet as it lashed back on its hinges and banged against the wooden side of the shed.

'Are you there, Tom?' she called. Where was he? Reaching out blindly in front of her, her fingers touched his thin jacket. She shook him. 'Wake up, our Tom! Wake up! I've got to get you inside.'

The boy stirred and stumbled to his feet. 'I'm s-so c-cold,' he stammered, his teeth rattling.

'Come on. Hang on to my arm,' Ellen

commanded him. 'I'll soon get you into t'warmth.'

She half carried, half dragged him across the yard to the kitchen door. 'Sit on the edge of the fender, Tom, while I bolt the door. Now, we've got to be quiet. I'll make you some gruel; that should help to warm you up. And here's some bread left over. I don't think Cook will miss a couple o' slices. And well take this old rug out of the pantry into the shed, when you have to go back. That should keep some of the cold off you and it won't look out of place, if someone sees it tomorrow. And there's an old coat hanging in the other outhouse. I'll go and get it now and bring it in here, to warm it up for you.'

Tom gratefully drank the hot gruel, clutching his hands around the outside of the mug to bring some warmth back into them. He speedily ate two slices of buttered toast, wiping the butter that dripped down his chin, with the back of his hand. 'That were good, our Ellen,' he thanked her, a bit of colour coming back into his face. 'I can't get over how growed up you look.'

His eyes lingered over her. 'I missed you so much after you'd gone, and our stepdad got wilder and wilder wi' me. He hits our mam, too – but she won't let me tell anyone. I'd have left sooner, only I didn't want to leave our mam.' He looked earnestly at her. 'I wouldn't have left now, only Mam told me to get away while I could. She was feared he'll kill me in one of his rages.'

Ellen hugged him. 'It's all right. I know you didn't desert her. I did the same, in a way.'

'I can't go back there, Ellen. I've got to find work, so as I can manage by meself. I know I can't stay 'ere. I don't want you getting into trouble on my account. I'll be off, as soon as I can.'

Ellen put her arms around him again. 'We'll manage as long as we need to,' she promised him. 'Now tell me a bit about all the others.'

Tom talked and Ellen asked questions, as the two of them sat huddled in front of the fire. Neither realized that they were falling asleep. Their eyelids grew heavy and, leaning one against the other, they drifted off into a deep sleep...

Eleven

It was the sound of someone being sick that stirred Ellen. For a moment, she wondered where she was. Then, as her senses came back to her, she jumped up in alarm.

It was Goldie, leaning over a bucket, who had disturbed her slumber. She was as startled as Ellen. She wiped her mouth on the back of her hand. 'What on earth are you doing here, Ellen?' she demanded. 'And who's that? I've heard of cradle-snatching but he's a bit young, even for you.'

'It's our Tom. He's run away from our stepdad. He kept beating him and kicking him. He wants to find work. Don't tell anyone, will you? He only needs a couple of days. I thought I might ask around for him; see if any of the traders who come here need an extra lad.'

'Well, you'd better get rid of him quick before anyone else comes down,' Goldie advised. 'I shan't tell on you but Cook might feel she has to.'

Ellen hurriedly shook Tom awake. 'Come

on, Tom. Wake up. It's morning. You'll have to go. Here, take this bread with you.' She quickly spread some butter on it and added a spoonful of jam. 'I'll put this rug in the shed for tonight. Go on, before someone comes and sees you.'

She pushed him towards the door and went out into the yard with him. 'I'll see you tonight,' she promised him. 'Try to find somewhere warm to shelter. Off you go, now.'

They had moved none too soon. Cook was in the kitchen when she returned indoors. 'My! You're up bright and early!' she exclaimed. 'Though I can't see what you've done. The fire's not lit, nor the kettle on the boil. Come on, get yourself moving.'

She noticed the empty plate. 'I can see you've had your breakfast. So go and help Goldie to get things ready in the dining room for their breakfasts up there. She still looks a bit peaky.' She busied herself getting some pans down. 'Get on with it, Ellen. Don't stand there looking as if you've seen a ghost. You'll be needed upstairs for Miss Sarah, soon. Don't forget, Mrs Oldfield and Miss Sarah are going to Manchester to choose some more going-away clothes. They'll be wanting either you or Nora to go with them to carry their parcels. Mr Fairchild's coming later on, so his room will need preparing, too. I'd better get Goldie to do that.'

Nora was chosen to go to Manchester, so Ellen did most of the upstairs work, Goldie keeping out of the way once she had tidied Mrs Oldfield's room and seen to Mr Fairchild's.

'What's the matter with her?' Doris wanted to know.

'I think she's got an upset stomach. She was being sick earlier on. I'll ask Cook if she can go to back to bed. I can cover the rest of her jobs.'

Mrs Garland made no objections. She had been pleased with Goldie's work since she had become a 'tweeny' again. She'd got over her disappointment very well and it wasn't like her to be off colour like this.

Ellen found her upstairs, coming out of Mr Fairchild's room.

Goldie jumped when she saw Ellen. 'I was just finishing off in there,' she hastened to explain. 'Ugh. I need to get back downstairs but the smell of food makes me feel sick again.' She clutched at her stomach, as she spoke.

Ellen told her of Mrs Garland's approval of a rest in bed for her. 'So, go on. Have a lie down,' she urged. 'I'll bring a hot brick for you, as soon as I can. I'll make sure all your work gets done.'

Goldie dropped her eyes. 'There's no need,' she muttered.

'I don't mind, honestly. I'll get you some thin gruel. You might be able to keep it down. You really do look peaky, Goldie.'

Goldie muttered, 'Thanks,' and made her way upstairs, one hand to her stomach and the other to her mouth.

Ellen rushed through the rest of her work and some of Goldie's and, as soon as she could, took a hot brick wrapped in old towels up to her. 'Here you are, Goldie. Let me put this brick in with you. You don't look at all well. Do you think you need to see a doctor?'

'Stop fussing me!' Goldie snapped. 'I'll be all right!'

'All right, all right. Keep your hair on!'

Ellen crouched at the side of the bed and felt under the mattress where she kept her wages until she was able to go to the bank. She could give the money to Tom. It would help him until he got a job. She slipped the cloth purse into the pocket of her frock and then took off her apron and unhooked her coat from the clothes rail.

'I thought you were staying in for your

afternoon off?' Goldie said, suddenly sounding more awake.

'I can't. I need to ask around for a job for our Tom.'

For some reason Ellen couldn't fathom, Goldie looked a bit agitated.

'What's the matter? Are you going to be sick again?'

'No, but I've just remembered I didn't put clean towels out in Mr Fairchild's room. I'd best go and do it.'

'Stay there; I'll do it,' Ellen offered. It was the least she could do; Goldie hadn't spilled on their Tom being there. She hung her coat up again as she spoke, glad to see Goldie sink back against her pillow.

'Did you know Mr John's coming home tomorrow?' Goldie asked as she reached the doorway.

Ellen turned back. 'No, I didn't. Are you sure?'

Hope flared within her. He'd help her find a job for their Tom, she was sure. But Goldie's next words shook her.

'He's bringing a young lady with him.'

'Oh!' Ellen's heart lurched and her face flushed. 'I didn't know. Who is it? Do we know her?'

'Ah! Feeling your nose pushed out, are

224

you?' Goldie taunted, her spirit reviving a little. 'She's his lady friend and she's called Miss Armstrong. According to Mrs Oldfield, we'll be seeing quite a lot of her.'

'Oh!' Ellen turned away so that Goldie couldn't see her face. So much for John's undying love! What was it about her that made men promise their love and leave her?

She hurried out of the room, leaving Goldie to her own thoughts as she turned her flushed face to the wall.

Ellen went to the linen store and selected a couple of towels to put in Mr Fairchild's room, trying to digest the unwelcome news Goldie had just told her. How close a friend was this Miss Armstrong? John hadn't mentioned her. Did he care deeply for her?

Although she had turned down his offer to take her back to Cambridge with him, it had been comforting to know he cared for her; and there were times when she wondered if she had acted too hastily. It might have worked, between them. They did get on well together. Well, it was too late for that, now!

As she pushed open the bedroom door, her mind was full of tumbling thoughts. She entered the room, surprised to see Mr Fairchild's toiletry items set out on the small bedside cabinet. She frowned. He must have decided to start leaving them here. She put the towels on the end of the bed but, as she turned back towards the door, the door began to swing closed revealing Mr Fairchild leaning nonchalantly against the wall behind it.

She stepped away, the palms of her hands ready to ward him off. 'What are you doing here? You aren't due till later.'

Her eyes darted back to the door but before she could move towards it, Fairchild pushed it closed.

'There's no need to rush away,' he drawled, moving closer. 'Stay a while ... and get to know me a bit better. After Christmas, we'll be living in the same house. It will make life so much more pleasant if we already know each other well, don't you think?' He smiled in satisfaction. 'There's no need to be afraid.'

A chill struck Ellen's stomach; she was very much afraid. 'I ... I haven't time. There's work to be done.' She glanced towards the door, wishing she was nearer to it.

Mr Fairchild wagged his finger at her. 'Come, come! We both know the ladies have gone out and Nora and Cadman have gone with them.'

'Doris is coming to help me! She'll be here soon!'

Mr Fairchild shook his head. 'Dear me, more lies. There's no use pretending. No one is coming and no one who matters knows I am here.' His words were softly spoken. 'And no one knows that you are here either.'

Ellen clutched at straws. 'Mrs Garland will wonder where I am. We're busy today! John is coming home tomorrow and–'

'And it's your half-day off! No one will miss you for hours.'

A deep chill clutched at Ellen's heart. It was true: no one would miss her ... except for Goldie! 'Goldie knows I'm here. She'll wonder why I've not gone back to her.'

'I don't think so.' He carelessly reached towards her and flicked a curl to one side. 'You could learn quite a lot from dear Goldie, Harris. I'm sure she'll be willing to teach you the way to please me.'

Ellen had backed up against the wall, fearful that her legs would fold beneath her. This couldn't be happening! She felt paralyzed by fear.

Fairchild put one hand upon the wall at the side of her head, blocking her way of escape. He drew the backs of the fingers of his other hand across her cheek. 'Such beautiful, soft skin,' he murmured, 'and such beautiful hair.' He plucked at her cap and it came away in his hand. 'I could buy you such pretty ornaments for your hair.' He stroked his hand over her shining curls. 'You would want for nothing!'

His touch made her flesh crawl. She knocked his hand away. 'I don't want anything from you! Get out and leave me to do my work!' Her voice was cold with fury and fear.

'Oh-oh! The lady fights back, does she? Come on, arouse my ardour some more!'

Ellen tried to control her whirling thoughts. Her throat felt tight and dry. She shivered as he reached out to touch her face again. She felt sick but summoned her reserves of strength into her voice. 'I really must insist that you let me return to my duties,' she snapped in bravado. 'Miss Sarah won't be pleased when I tell her!'

'Oh-oh! And what exactly do you propose to say to my delectable fiancée? I shall deny it all, except, maybe, to say that I found you in my room lying unclothed on my bed; waiting for me.' He smiled persuasively. 'Come on, Harris ... or should I say, Ellen? Let's start with a kiss. That's harmless enough. Your lips are very tempting, don't you know. I bet lots of lads have savoured your sweet kisses, eh?' He leaned forwards as he lowered his head.

'No!'

She tried to push him away but her strength was no match for his. She could feel his tongue running along her lips, trying to push its way into her mouth. His other hand found her breast and squeezed it hard.

She gasped in shock. A moan sounded within her mouth but she knew it hadn't come from her. She felt nausea gagging in her throat and twisted her head away.

Fairchild laughed. He tried to draw her towards the bed but Ellen pulled away. If she could just get to the door ... but Fairchild was stronger. He dragged her forward and pushed her backwards onto the bed, dropping on top of her.

She screamed and struggled to free herself. But it was impossible. He was too strong, too heavy. She opened her mouth to scream again but Fairchild clapped a hand over it before she had uttered a sound.

'There's no one to hear you ... but, in case you still think it is worth a try, think about your brother being taken to prison.'

Ellen froze. How did he know? Her spirit sank. Goldie had told him!

'I know all about him,' Fairchild continued. 'How you have hidden him in the woodshed, stolen food for him, taken a coat out of the kitchen. I wonder what your un-suspecting employers will think of that?'

He released his hand from her mouth but still sat astride her, laughing triumphantly. 'You see! I know all about you. I know what goes on inside your pretty little head. You're all the same, you serving wenches, beguiling us men; fluttering your eyes at us.'

'That's not true!'

She struggled to free herself. She could see his open cut-throat razor lying on top of the bedside table. She tried to reach for it but Fairchild caught hold of her wrist.

'No, you don't!' he snarled.

She could feel his other hand roughly fumbling and pulling at her drawers. His action rekindled her resistance.

'No!' She tore the nails of her free hand across his cheeks, drawing blood.

'Wildcat!' he spat at her, viciously slapping her face back and forth, until she felt numbed by terror. 'If you want to play rough, I'll show you how rough I can be!'

As she jerked her head from side to side in a futile effort to avoid the stinging blows, her hair cascaded across the pillow. 'Help! Someone, help me!'

She clawed at his face. She wouldn't be the only one with bruises! But it only made him slap her harder. He was insane. Her face would be bruised. Did he think no one would notice? She was momentarily winded. Her head felt strange, as if she were suffocating. Memories of her stepfather flooded back as her skirt was bunched up to her waist and her drawers wrenched away. 'Stop! Please stop!'

But he didn't. He forced his way between her legs. It was her nightmare come true. She was a child again, unable to resist her stepfather's assaults. But it was worse. She felt defiled; dirty; degraded. She groaned in despair, the fight at last drained out of her.

The door crashed open and a shrill voice demanded, 'What is going on?'

Fairchild jerked to a standstill as an appalling silence sliced into the room.

Ellen felt a mixture of relief and shame as she saw Mrs Oldfield framed in the doorway, shock and disbelief distorting her face. Behind her, their faces showing bewilderment, stood John, Miss Sarah and another lady.

Fairchild's face changed colour. His manly ardour shrivelled away, as he hastily scrambled off the bed, frantically trying to rearrange his clothing, fastening his buttons, as he cowered before them. 'You're back!' he faltered. 'Er ... I can explain... She ... er ...

taunted me. She's no better than—'

His next words went unheard, as a terrible scream rent from Miss Sarah's mouth; a scream like that of a wounded animal. As the sound gurgled away, she slipped to the floor.

John leapt forwards in an uncontrolled rage. 'Animal! Animal!' A well-aimed blow knocked Fairchild to the floor. John fell on top of him, raining blow upon blow against him.

Ellen made an effort to push her skirt down, as Mrs Oldfield, her face contorted with anger, approached the bed.

'You vixen!' she spat. 'You whore! Betraying your mistress in this disgusting way!'

Ellen stared at Mrs Oldfield, unable to make sense of what she was hearing.

John paused in his effort of trying to haul Fairchild to his feet. 'Hey, hang on, Mama!' he protested. 'She's hardly to blame for all this. It's Fairchild who needs to be dealt with, not Ellen!'

His use of her Christian name was not lost on his mother. She ignored his protests. Miss Sarah was reviving at her feet. 'Take the two ladies away, John,' she coldly requested. 'I will deal with what we have here.'

'Let me help her, Mama,' John implored, making a move forward.

Mrs Oldfield placed herself between her son and the girl lying on the bed. 'Leave this to me, John!' Her voice was like ice. 'When you have settled the ladies, go straight to the works and bring your father home immediately.'

As John reluctantly ushered his sister and Miss Armstrong out of the room, Fairchild struggled unaided to his feet, tenderly rubbing his jaw. 'Look, this isn't what it seems! You know what serving maids are like.'

The look on Mrs Oldfield's face quelled his words. 'I suggest you get yourself properly dressed, Mr Fairchild, and wait downstairs in the drawing room until my husband comes to see you and hears what explanation you have to offer!'

Ellen had managed to push her skirt down to cover her shame. The late afternoon gloom hung over the room but she wished it were completely dark. A mixture of emotions hurtled through her mind; shame at being seen like this; relief that the ordeal was over; and apprehension of what would happen next. She couldn't stay here; not after this. But where could she go?

Her employer's face hovered over her, her eyes bulging, her mouth contorted. 'You whore! You scheming, good-for-nothing baggage!' Mrs Oldfield's voice hissed through the air, flecks of spittle spraying from her mouth. 'How dare you ruin my daughter's life like this?'

Froth of more spittle gathered on her lips. 'Thank goodness we met up with my son and his young lady at Bolton railway station and decided to come back with them! That tore your scheming plans to shreds, didn't it? Ha! The look of guilt on your face!' she crowed in triumph, thrusting her face nearer.

The sight of Ellen's unrestrained hair increased her anger. 'I knew you were trouble from the start, flaunting your hair, even as a child! You deserve to be flogged for what you've done! Do you hear! Flogged!'

Ellen recoiled as the enraged woman lifted her hand, Fairchild's belt looped in it. She curled into a ball, taking the blows on her undefended back, as lash after lash rained upon her.

There was a brief pause but Ellen was too exhausted to move. When she felt her hair grabbed, her eyes flew open to see the cut-throat razor in Mrs Oldfield's hand.

'No!'

But it was her hair that was being attacked, not her throat. Handful after handful hacked off and flung onto the floor.

'We'll see what they think of you now!' Mrs Oldfield said grimly, still gripping the razor in her clenched fist.

Ellen read in her crazed eyes what her next move was to be. She screamed and tried to scrabble to the far side of the bed, but her strength seemed to have ebbed away.

A startled shout from the doorway, halted the scene.

'Mother!'

John rushed across the room and snatched the razor from his mother's grip. His eyes took in the torn clothing and the tousled chopped mess of her hair.

'What have you done, Mother?' he whispered in shock. He pushed her aside and gathered Ellen into his arms, dropping the razor onto the bed. 'Oh, my poor darling.' He stroked her hair and down her cheek. 'Why, Mother? Why?'

Ellen lay still in his arms; she ached and hurt beyond belief. Her body screamed with pain yet her mind was numbed.

John rocked her back and forth, as one would rock a child in need of comfort.

'Put her down!' his mother screamed at him. 'Put that slut down at once!'

John looked at her in anger. 'How can you say that, when you saw what happened here?

Fairchild was raping her! Can't you see that? Can't you hear what I am saying?'

'She must have asked for it! I shall cast her out on the street where she belongs. A guttersnipe, that's all she is!'

'No, Mother. No! I will marry her first!' He looked down at Ellen. 'I love you, Ellen. I only brought Grace home to make you jealous. Come away with me. We'll be married as soon as we can. I'll take care of you.'

Ellen listened in bewilderment as mother and son shouted at each other. John's earnest pleading didn't convey much meaning. His mother's screamed words were incoherent.

'Marry her? How dare you say that to me? You will never disgrace us like that! Never! Do you hear? I'll kill her!' Mrs Oldfield raised her hand, the razor once more in her grip.

Ellen saw the flash of steel as it descended.

A scream arose in her throat but, when the scream came, it wasn't from her ... and the flesh that was torn wasn't hers, either.

Twelve

As John collapsed on top of her, another scream tore through the air.

'My son! You've killed my son!'

Ellen rolled aside and grabbed at the hand that held the bloodied razor so that it merely scratched along her neck towards her shoulder.

The screaming continued as the frenzied woman collapsed onto her son.

Ellen twisted away and scrambled off the bed. She looked at the blood spreading upon the white sheets, and the woman, sobbing hysterically. John's face was white and still. Had his mother killed him?

What could she do? Who would believe her? She must go! Away from this madness. She backed to the open doorway, her horrified eyes fixed on the mother and son.

'I loved you, John! I'd have come with you!'

She felt the carved wood of the doorframe under her fingers and she turned and fled from the room. Along the corridor she ran, pushing past the startled figure of Miss

237

Armstrong, who was coming back to see if there was anything she could do. The bewildered woman flattened herself against the wall as the fleeing figure rushed past her.

Ellen passed the servants' door. It was closed – but it didn't lead to safety, anyway. They couldn't shield an accused murderess. And that would be the accusation! The words, 'You've killed my son!' still rang in her ears.

She ran on. More screams and shouts echoed from the bedroom, spurring her on to the top of the main staircase. Again she paused, uncertain what to do then her feet continued her flight down the stairs. The front door was swinging open, left unfastened by Bert when John had urged him to go as quickly as he could to the brickworks to bring Mr Oldfield home. With no regard for the coldness of the air and the sleeting rain, she ran through the doorway and down the front steps.

She ran, stumbling, not knowing where she was going. She turned up Chapel Lane towards Chorley Old Road, away from the brickworks. The rain stung her face. Her torn clothes clung to her, sticking to her form, giving no warmth or protection. Why hadn't she stopped to get her coat? Goldie was probably asleep and wouldn't have heard her. She hesitated – but she didn't dare go back.

She had to get away. But where could she go?

Her mam! She wanted her mam! But she couldn't go there. Zach Durban was there.

Her throat hurt. The rain lashed down upon her upturned face, driving into her mouth, running down her neck and down her body. 'Charlie! Where are you, Charlie?' she groaned. 'Charlie! I need you!'

But he'd forgotten her, hadn't he?

Grandma, then. She must get to Grandma! But how? She'd no money. And Tom ... where was Tom? He'd be coming back tonight. He might be hanging around the railway station. She could try there.

She turned and stumbled down Church Street towards the railway station. Two people were coming towards her, a man and a boy, both with their heads down against the sleet. She shrank away from them and almost let them pass by but, at the last moment, she recognized her brother. 'Tom?'

'Ellen?'

They stopped and gaped at each other.

'What yer doing out in this, Ellen? I was coming to tell yer I've got a job. Mr Hart's fireman's lad got a better job and he said I can take his place, and Mr Hart, 'ere, has said I can live with him and his missus for half me wage!' His face looked jubilant for a moment but faded into a look of concern. 'But, what's up, Ellen? You don't 'alf look a mess! What's happened to yer hair? And yer frock's torn.'

Ellen clasped her hands to her head. She'd forgotten that part of it; and she was soaking wet. She couldn't go anywhere like this!

'Mrs Oldfield did it. She ... she...' What could she say in front of this stranger? 'I've got to get away. I can't go back, Tom. I can't!'

The man with Tom was shrugging off his jacket. 'Here, lass, wrap this round yer,' he said, putting it across her shoulders.

Ellen felt too cold to protest. She was shivering violently.

'T'best thing you can do, lass, is to come home wi' me and your brother. Me missus'll sort you out and give you summat hot to put inside yer.'

'I can't! Mrs Oldfield'll get the police! She'll say–'

'Have yer done owt wrong, lass?' the man asked bluntly.

Ellen shook her head. 'No, but she'll say–'

'Ne'er mind what she'll say. Come 'ome

with us. Well see you're all reet afore you go on yer way.'

Ellen felt too dazed to resist. With the man's arm around her shoulders and Tom on the other side of her, she stumbled along between them through some streets of the town she knew led to the market. They stopped partway along Winter Street, where the man pushed open a door and hustled her inside, calling out, 'Are yer there, Alice? Get t'kettle on, will yer? I've a lass here who needs summat warm inside her.'

Ellen let herself be guided through to the back room. After one glance at the state of her, the woman he'd called Alice ushered out the men and, in a matter of minutes, Ellen was stripped out of her wet clothes. After gasping at the bruised state of her body, Alice gently smoothed some soothing balm on her upper body and then wrapped her gently in a blanket and seated her by the fire.

Ellen could barely think. Everything around her seemed enveloped in a hazy mist. She sipped at the mug of hot tea that was thrust into her hands but couldn't make sense of the words that were being spoken around her. She was finally helped up the wooden staircase and put into a narrow bed that had been warmed with a stone hot-water bottle.

'Your Tom was goin' to sleep 'ere,' she heard Mrs Hart say, 'but he can bed down in t'kitchen for a night or two. Now get yerself some shut-eye and yer'll be as reet as rain in t'morning.'

Ellen doubted that. She'd never be as right as rain again.

It was a week before Ellen felt able to get dressed in her frock that Mrs Hart had mended and washed for her. She was in a state of shock and she stared blankly when Mrs Hart ministered to her bodily needs and smoothed more balm onto her bruised flesh.

She couldn't even face their Tom. She felt defiled and shamed and wanted to hide away from mankind. However, Ellen knew she would have to tell them at least part of what had happened. They'd been so kind to her and to Tom. Mrs Hart had even tidied up her hair with a pair of scissors. It was only right that they knew what she was facing – and what they would be facing as well if they continued to shield her from the police.

She gripped hold of the banister rail as she went down the stairs into the small kitchen. Mrs Hart fussed about her, making sure she was warm by the fire. She gave her a mug of

broth, cajoling her to sip at it; talking soothing words as if to a child, expecting no reply;
understanding that the words to explain what
had happened would be difficult to express.

'In your own time, love,' she murmured,
whenever Ellen looked at her with panic in
her eyes.

Haltingly, Ellen told them what had
happened; not all the details, of course, but
enough to make them understand why she
had to get away.

'Well, we can put yer mind at rest that
nob'dy got killed,' Mr Hart assured her. 'I
listened around a bit, to see what I could
find out. There was talk of some shenanigans going on up yon, 'cos t'doctor were
called. All t'surgery heard about it. It's being
said t'young man fell down t'stairs wi' a
knife in his hand. Seems he nearly slashed
his arm off and lost a lot of blood but he'll
recover. T'rest seems to have been hushed
up. There's no one looking for you, lass; at
least, not t'police.'

Ellen was relieved – both that John was
alive and that she would not be accused of
murder. Knowing Mrs Oldfield, though, she
knew some sort of accusation would be
made against her. She still needed to get
away. She felt shamed and dirty.

She stayed a few more days, her mind and body being healed by the kindness meted out to her. She wrote a short letter to her grandma, asking if she could go to her and the reply came, assuring her of her welcome. On the following Friday evening, Mr Hart told her he'd volunteered to do a double shift the next day.

'So, when I get to Bolton, someone else brings my engine back here and I take another on to Manchester Victoria,' he explained. 'So, if that's where you want to go, lass, I'll see you get there safely.'

Mrs Hart had found Ellen's purse in the pocket of her frock and had bought some pieces of underwear for her from the second-hand stall on the market. She also bought her a warm coat, a bonnet and muffler. There was enough left over to give the kind woman some money towards her food and lodgings. Not that it was asked for, but it salved Ellen's pride.

She felt sad to be leaving Horwich. She'd lived here nine years and the first eight years had been happy. Only the past year had left scars on her life.

They changed trains at Bolton and then travelled on to Salford, past row upon row of terraced houses clustered around towering factories and mills. Everything looked drab and grey, covered by the pall of smoke from thousands of chimneys. What a contrast to the green fields and moors around Horwich.

She got off the train at Salford, hugged Tom, shook hands with Mr Hart and, choking back tears, made her way to the exit. And there was Grandma, waiting just beyond the ticket barrier. Ellen flung herself into her open arms. How she had missed her wise counsel over the recent few years!

'And me mam? Will I see me mam?'

Dorcas nodded. 'She'll come as soon as she can. Let's go home. Lizzie will have the kettle on.'

They made their way through the streets of the inner city. The buildings seemed to press in from all sides. She'd forgotten the dirt, the smells of the city; the rows upon rows of chimneys belching out polluted smoke, covering everywhere and everyone with a grimy layer of soot. It tasted on their tongues and smarted their eyes. The streets were strewn with litter and bordered by gutters running with filth.

City noises rang in her ears; the ring of steel-banded wheels on the stone-cobbled roads; the ill-matched clopping of horses' hoofs and the growl of the new motorized engines that now invaded the city centre; the shouts of vendors; women calling and arguing; children's cries, as they played or fought, children whose wide eyes stared out of their dirty faces.

But all of that was better than the sullen silence from the many grown men who lounged in the shop doorways or leaned against the lamp posts. Their hostile stares began to alarm her and she pulled her muffler more firmly around her neck and over her mouth, as if to keep the smells and tastes at bay. She clutched Grandma's arm and pressed closer to her.

'Why aren't they at work?' she asked.

'Times are hard. There are many such in all the towns and cities. Keep your eyes down, then you won't attract their attention as much.'

As they walked on, Ellen was glad to see the streets were becoming less crowded, though the heavy pall of smoke was ever present. She'd never been to this part of the city. It was the opposite side of Manchester from where she had grown up ... and far away from her stepfather.

She recognized the name of the street and began to count the numbers on the doors. 'Twelve, fourteen, sixteen.' Not much further. As they neared number twenty-six, a mixture of emotions rushed around inside of her. It was such a long time since she had seen any of her family except Tom and Grandma. Would she recognize them? The door opened.

There was silence for a moment or two, as the two young women stared at each other. It was her cousin Lizzie. Ellen was the first to gain her voice.

'Lizzie! Oh, Lizzie! It's good to see you again!'

A smile lit Lizzie's face, as she held out her arms. 'Ellen!' The two cousins hugged each other in delight. Lizzie drew Ellen into the house, then held her at arm's length. 'Eeh! You've certainly growed and filled out,' she admired. 'Eeh, wait till the others see you!'

At the sound of their voices, a group of children appeared in the doorway to the kitchen. A lump came into Ellen's throat at the sight of them.

Hesitantly, the children moved forward but then stood shyly a little way from her, their clean, scrubbed faces a vast difference from the children they had passed by in the city centre.

'Come on. Say "hello" to Ellen,' Dorcas urged them.

Ellen knew the two youngest were Lizzie's own, born since Grandma had moved back to live with them, allowing Lizzie to marry her sweetheart, Norman. Some of the others were Lizzie's younger brothers and sisters. It wasn't them her eyes were searching for. She was looking for her own sisters ... and there they were: Flossie, her lips pouting slightly and a wary look in her eyes, and Maud, self-conscious but grinning with delight.

Ellen smiled at them and held out her arms. 'Come and hug me. Gosh, how grown up you are, Flossie! And you, too, Maud.'

'I'm nearly fifteen,' Flossie announced importantly. 'I've left school and I work in Norman's dad's shop a couple of days every week.' She tossed back her hair and stood proudly, her stance challenging.

Ellen noted her jutting chin and the way the back of her hands rested on her hips. 'That's lovely,' she said, recognizing her sister's fear of being displaced from her position as 'elder' sister.

'And I'm eleven and a half,' Maud told her. 'I leave school next summer. I'll be able to get a job then.'

Her two brothers, Jack and Herbie, weren't there. Grandma had already explained that it would make Zach Durban suspicious if all of his family were suddenly missing. She'd see them another day; and her mam was coming later.

Tears filled her eyes. She tried to blink them away but they ran freely down her cheeks. Dorcas enveloped her in her arms once more, hardly conscious that her own tears were falling onto Ellen's bonnet. 'There, there, my dear. You're safe at home now.'

Home!

It was – yet it wasn't! She didn't really have a home. Her mam's home was a couple of miles away – where her mam and brothers – and that man – still lived. She could no more go there than she could return to Horwich, her home of the past nine years. Her mam! She gulped back the longing that threatened to overcome her. She might be nineteen – but she still needed her mam!

'What we need is a cup of tea,' Dorcas said decisively. 'Come on, girls. Get the kettle on.'

Glad that the strained awkwardness of the tearful reunion was over, a babble of voices broke out around her. Flossie's decisive tones: 'I'll make t'tea. Come and put t'cakes out, our Maud.' And the little ones, catching the excitement, clapped their hands and jumped about the room.

'Did you have to do this at the Oldfields'?' Maud asked shyly, as she brought in a plate of cakes. What was it like in the big house? Did you wear a special frock? I'd like to be a maid. I like making tea ... only not somewhere where they'd be unkind to me.'

Ellen smiled as she accepted a piece of cake, knowing that was all the younger ones knew. 'It wasn't all bad. I enjoyed it. I'll tell you all about it another time.'

Later, in the evening, when the children were in bed, the adults settled round the hearth to hear in greater detail what had happened. Flossie had protested long and loud about how unfair it was that she and Maud had to go up with the children. She wasn't a child! Why couldn't she hear all about it too? But Grandma insisted and Flossie flounced upstairs behind the others.

A small fire had been lit in the grate. Ellen held out her hands towards it. The glowing fire gave comfort – somewhere to stare with unseeing eyes when the pain of the memories was almost too much to bear. The orange and red flames danced and flickered; the smoke curled and twisted as it was drawn up the chimney.

The listeners were also thankful for somewhere to look when they were afraid to look straight into Ellen's eyes, helpless to offer anything other than words of distress or comfort. Their murmured words were enough. Their comfort wrapped itself around her like a shawl and it strengthened her.

Ada Durban was there now, summoned by Norman on the pretext of 'one o't'bairns is took bad. Can yer come?' Almost thrown out of her house, she was, Zach loud in his displeasure. '... And get yer b– self back 'ere fast, woman. I want me rights.'

They sat immobile, except for the drift of their eyes, as they heard what had happened. Ada clasped her daughter's hands tightly in her own, not knowing if they were her tears, or Ellen's, that splashed down onto them. Norman sat on the arm of Lizzie's chair, his arm around her shoulders, as if to protect her from anything similar that might threaten her.

'Oh, dear Lord! What did we send you to?' Ada cried out. Her hands flew involuntarily to cover the lower part of her face. 'Oh! My poor baby! I shouldn't 'ave let you go, only...! Oh, Lord!' Her voice dropped into a whisper and her face contorted itself as her mind played out the scene in her imagination.

She hated this man, Fairchild; she hated

Zach Durban; she hated all the men who took advantage of their womenfolk. The ball of hate churned around in her body – in her stomach; in her heart; in her lungs. And when it swelled and became too much to bear, she opened her mouth and it tore from her in a sound of animal-like pain that stemmed from the lava of hate that surged and roared within her.

It broke the spell that bound the others, jerking them into reality with a sense of shock that they could hardly comprehend.

Ellen was the first to move. 'Mam! Don't! Don't! I can't bear it!' She leapt from her seat and threw her arms around her mam, hugging her to her breast, rocking her backwards and forwards. 'It's all gone, Mam. I'm all right, honest ... I am.'

Dorcas rose also and enveloped them both, murmuring, 'Hush, dears. Hush.' Her voice was barely heard but her soothing sounds were as balm to their souls. Ada's cries subsided to sobs and the tension eased.

'What's the matter with our mam?'

Flossie's voice startled them all. They stared at her, themselves still shaken by Ada's distress. It was Lizzie who ran over to her.

'Flossie! Flossie, love! It's all right. She's upset, that's all.'

Flossie's eyes blazed. She pointed accusingly at Ellen. 'It's her, isn't it? Our Ellen! What right 'as she to come back 'ere, upsetting our mam like this?'

Ellen stared helplessly at her sister. What could she say? 'I'm sorry. I didn't mean to–'

'Why don't yer get back where yer've come from and leave us alone? We don't need you 'ere. You'll be tekin' my place, I know.'

'That's quite enough, Flossie! Go back upstairs and I will speak to you in the morning.' Dorcas spoke sternly and would brook no nonsense. She felt sorry for Flossie. She knew she was extremely distressed but her presence and attitude really wasn't making it any easier for any of them.

'But...!'

'Go, now!'

Flossie defiantly set her mouth in a straight line and narrowed her eyes. She looked as if she would speak again, but thought better of it. She turned on her heels and left the room, slamming the door behind her. They heard her footsteps as she stamped her way up each stair and the eventual slam of the bedroom door, followed by a wail from one of the little ones.

'It's all right. I'll go.' Lizzie slipped quietly upstairs, leaving the others to look at each other in consternation.

Ellen's spirit sank. Her coming here was going to cause as many problems as it might solve. But where else could she go?

Thirteen

Over the next few days, Ada came each day, supposedly to tend to the 'sick child'. She also brought news of Jack and Herbie, now aged thirteen and ten, respectively. 'I daren't bring them to see you, in case they let slip to Zach that you are here. He still blames all of his problems on you. I dread to think what he'd do if he knew you were back so near.'

It hurt that part of her family were still denied to her but Ellen knew it was for the best. It wasn't only Zach Durban she feared but men in general. She knew it was illogical. Most men lived life as decently as they could – but how could she know which might harm her? Her dazed mind seemed incapable of coping with the dilemma and she spent most of her days huddled by the kitchen fire. Life went on around her but it seemed not to touch her. Dorcas and Lizzie

254

tried to rouse her out of it but with little success. She did any household jobs they asked of her but her vitality was gone.

Ada came as often as she could and Ellen would lean against her on the sofa, drawing comfort from her presence, reliving memories from her childhood.

Just before Christmas, Dorcas received a letter from John Oldfield. He apologized for the delay in writing but explained that he had only just managed to discover Ellen's new postal address. He wrote briefly about the circumstances of Ellen's hasty departure from Horwich, expressing his desire to find where she had gone, imploring Dorcas to let him know if Ellen had made contact with her. He said he had been convalescing and was returning to Cambridge in the New Year.

Ellen didn't know how to respond. Her mind couldn't grasp hold of what he was saying. The whole episode had been so traumatic she couldn't yet face thinking about it.

Dorcas didn't force her to make a decision.

Christmas was celebrated quietly. Lizzie and Norman took some of the children to church but Ellen hadn't yet been beyond the front door and had no desire to face any well-meant seasonal greetings from strangers. She remained in the house to help her grandma cook a Christmas dinner that did justice to the occasion. It was lovely to be with her family. Everyone had bought or made little gifts for each other and the parlour games they played afterwards brought much laughter.

The coming of the New Year brought with it the promise of new beginnings. Ellen's bruised body was healing; but her bruised mind was taking longer. However, as the days lightened, she felt herself slowly coming out of what seemed like a period of dazedness. Her spirit began to feel lighter and she found herself beginning to look ahead.

She was nineteen years old. She had a lifetime ahead of her. She wasn't going to let men like Zach Durban and Leslie Fairchild rule her future just because they had despoiled her past. It was now 1910 – a new decade. King Edward VII was ailing and a new era would be beginning soon; Ellen suddenly realized she wanted to be part of it. Women who had stood up to demand their place in society throughout the previous decade would most surely be pushing forward for more.

She began to spend a few hours serving in Norman's shop but it quickly became apparent that Flossie resented her presence there.

Eager young men suddenly began to appear at the shop counter, their faces a bright shade of red as they tried to attract the new assistant's attention with their stumbling banter. They may as well have been speaking in a foreign language. Ellen wasn't interested.

Not that Flossie saw it that way. 'Ronnie Briggs was asking me out before you came along!' she accused in a shrill voice. 'Now you're egging him on to ask you! You always take what I've got! It's not fair! I wish you'd never come back!'

As well as causing trouble in that quarter, Ellen also knew that her presence stretched the family's resources to the limit. Dorcas, Norman and Lizzie all assured her that there was plenty of room for her and enough money to stretch to cover her food but it took the shine off her pleasure of being back with her family.

But, where else could she go? She didn't feel ready to make a new start anywhere else. What if the same sort of treatment was handed out again? She knew from Nora's experience that it was highly probable; whereas here she was safe – as long as she kept out of Zach Durban's way.

Maybe it was time to look for a job nearby, so that she could continue to live here.

Surely, no employer would molest her if she was living with her family? She wouldn't be as dependent upon them as a live-in servant was. And she had eyes in her head, didn't she? She would leave immediately if there was any sign of danger. She wouldn't let the past dominate her future any longer!

A surge of spirit sparked within her. She'd read pamphlets. Some women were taking charge of their own destinies these days. They weren't prepared to allow bullying men – or bullying women, for that matter – to destroy their lives. They were standing up and declaring their right to make decisions in matters that affected them.

So, what could she do?

She could cook and sew, but, thanks to John, she was also quite well educated for a young woman of her class. She was sure she would find an opening somewhere; an opening that promised a brighter future. If she didn't go near where Zach Durban lived, she'd be all right.

She began to take walks out every day, looking at handwritten advertisements in shop windows, going into the library to read the advertising section of the various newspapers, writing down the addresses of any jobs that seemed suited to her abilities.

There weren't many. There was too much unemployment in the outer city environs ... and men were given the first opportunities.

It also became obvious that if she wanted to get the sort of job that paid more than a shilling or two per week, she needed to be wearing something better than her present much-mended frock ... and her hair needed some attention. Her unruly curls, albeit tidier than they were before Christmas, wouldn't endear her to any prospective employers.

A visit to the local market with her grandma solved the first problem and she returned home with a frock made of dark blue grosgrain. It was smart enough to be fashionable and sensible enough to take her anywhere. A couple of plain skirts and two blouses completed her purchases and all they needed were a few simple adjustments to make them fit perfectly to her slim figure.

By the time Norman and Flossie were home from the shop the altered garments were hanging from the picture rail. Flossie eyed them darkly, comparing them to her own.

'Yours were new only last month,' Dorcas tactfully reminded her.

'Well, they're not as nice,' Flossie said with pouting lips. 'And they show me ankles.

They make me look like a child. It's embarrassing!'

'That's because you're growing up so fast,' Ellen tried to pacify her, 'but don't worry. I'll help you buy some more once I'm earning some money.'

Flossie brightened at once. 'I'll have emerald green or a rich ruby red,' she enthused. 'And if I put my hair up, I'll look every bit as old as Polly Saunders. That'll show her!'

Heads turned, both male and female, as Ellen made her way down the city street, even though she had pulled her hair back from her face, plastered it flat with a thin sugar solution and fastened it in a tight knot at the nape of her neck with a piece of brown ribbon and numerous pins. Whereas her outfit wasn't as grand as the bespoke creations that adorned the more wealthy, having watched Miss Sarah parade up and down the fitting rooms, she knew how to walk correctly and gracefully deport herself.

A number of prospective employers had already regretted that she didn't precisely fit their requirements. Refusing to lie about her lack of experience in the commercial world and the more academic studies, she knew that she fell short of their expectations.

But, today, she was following another lead, one she had overheard whilst she was reading the 'Situations Vacant' notice in a newspaper in the library. Two young men were searching for jobs listed in a different newspaper but when the word 'bookshop' was mentioned, Ellen's ears pricked up. A vacancy in a bookshop? Now that was something she would actually enjoy, as well as it being a means of earning her living.

As soon as the young men had moved away, she hurried over to where they had been sitting and there it was, circled in blue ink. Liptrot's Bookshop. She pulled out her scrap of paper and jotted down the address. Lunchtime was long past. She would go immediately.

At half past eight that morning, Mrs Harriet Liptrot had slowly made her way down the bare wooden stairs into what had been her late husband's bookshop. Those stairs got steeper every day, she was sure. It was as well she didn't have to go back upstairs until it was time for bed or she'd never make it. Life had been a bit difficult since that fall a few weeks ago. Lucky not to have broken her leg, the doctor said.

The following day, she had placed an

advertisement for an assistant in the local paper and awaited the appearance of an ideal young man ... one who could run up and down the ladders all day long, talk to the customers and be capable of understanding her late husband's adventurous system of bookkeeping. A lad of about nineteen would be ideal. Young enough to have the stamina, yet old enough to have a good knowledge and interest in Horace's precious books.

Two young men had already tried their luck that morning – and countless others in the past week. Plenty of energy, most of them had, she'd give them that. Too much energy, some of them! However, they had been lacking in her other requirements. One couldn't even read properly. What did they teach them in school these days? If this was what compulsory education up to the age of twelve did for them, then they'd do better to get back to the old days – and quick sharp!

The jangling bell interrupted her musings. She replaced the book she was trying to catalogue onto the stack of new deliveries that morning and looked over the top of her spectacles at the young woman who had entered the shop. The term 'schoolma'am' sprang to mind, though her features were fine. Now, what sort of book would she be after? Textbooks, no doubt ... though they did say that under many a prim exterior a fluttering heart did pound! Maybe it would be romances? Possibly the Gothic variety? She chuckled to herself. The books young women read these days! Still, it kept her in business, so she wouldn't complain.

'Good afternoon, miss. How may I help you?'

Ellen eyed her speculatively. If the owner already had a woman working in his shop, would that make him more likely to employ another? Or was he wanting to replace this rather elderly woman with a young man? Was he at work elsewhere in the shop? She glanced around but could neither see nor hear anyone else on the premises.

Ellen approached the woman behind the counter, aware that her tentative smile belied the fluttering sensation in her stomach. Suppose the job had already gone? Had the young men from the library got here before her?

But, enough of this prevaricating. She must pull herself together and speak out before she was written off as being somewhat lacking.

'Good afternoon, ma'am. Is the proprietor available? I would like to speak with him.'

'On what business?'

'I ... er ... saw the advertisement for an assistant. I'd like to apply for the job.'

The woman looked surprised.

'Would you, now? And what makes you think you would be a suitable applicant? This is a business I'm running. Not a play shop.'

Ellen couldn't help allowing her surprise to show on her face. 'You are the owner, ma'am? I thought that is, I expected...' She pressed her lips together, to prevent more stammering remarks from ruining her prospects before she even got around to stating her meagre credentials. Impulsively, she thrust forward her right hand. 'Then I am very pleased to hear it, ma'am. I, too, believe that we women are capable of much more than men, in general, give us credit for. I would count it an honour to work for you, ma'am.'

'So would many others, miss, but none of the applicants I have seen so far have convinced me of their worth. Why should I employ you? I need someone who understands books and who doesn't think it beneath them to be on their feet nearly all day; someone who is able to serve my customers intelligently and politely.'

'I know a lot about books, ma'am and

enjoy reading, myself. I'm sure I could do the job every bit as well as a boy or young man.'

'What sort of books? Romantic novels?'

Ellen's face fell. She hadn't read many romantic novels. They didn't figure largely in the Oldfield library, though she knew of such authors as Jane Austen and the Brontë sisters and Mrs Gaskell, among others. 'I have read most of the works of William Shakespeare,' she confessed, 'and Robert Louis Stevenson and John Galsworthy. Also many of the classic poets.'

'Have you, indeed? And what about non-fiction? Do you know anything about text-books, such as the young men at Victoria University might be wanting?'

'I could learn,' Ellen faltered. 'My previous employer had quite an extensive library and I was allowed to borrow his books.'

'Hmmph! Read this to me,' the woman said abruptly, handing her the book on top of the new delivery pile.

Ellen removed her gloves and carefully opened the book, taking care not to bend its spine. It was a book about fishing, with terms and names that were new to her but she read a passage as fluently as she was able.

'Suppose I was a customer and wanted to

know more about philately. How would you help me?' The woman's eyes gleamed with challenge.

Ellen glanced about her. 'I don't know exactly where you keep the books on stamp-collecting,' she mused, 'but I'm sure you keep fiction and non-fiction books separately and will have your books in some sort of alphabetical order, either by subject or author. It wouldn't take me long to learn your system, I'm sure.'

The woman thrust the opened ledger at her. 'I was about to enter that book when you came in. Write down on this piece of paper what you would enter for it.'

Ellen read what was in the existing columns and laid the piece of paper under the last entry. She took the proffered pen out of Mrs Liptrot's hand and carefully wrote the corresponding details in similar style. 'Is that what you require?'

'Hmm! What about those steps? I need someone agile enough to do that … without being in danger of falling.'

'I'm perfectly capable of climbing steps,' Ellen assured her. 'In my last job, I was running up and down stairs all day. I shall make a divided skirt as soon as I am able, so that every propriety is taken care of.'

Mrs Liptrot considered her response. At least she wasn't a spiritless female who would blush at every handsome young man who came into her shop. And, once word got around, she was sure young men would come to look at more than her books! Not that she would stand any nonsense from them – and, from the looks of her, neither would she!

She held out her hand. 'Then I shall be happy to take you on for a trial period! When can you start?'

Ellen glanced up at the clock on the wall. 'I can stay for an hour or so now,' she volunteered. 'I won't expect you to pay me for today, of course,' she said, thinking of Mrs Oldfield's 'training periods', 'but I'm sure I'll quickly pick up everything I need to know.'

Mrs Liptrot regarded her eager face shrewdly. 'I don't know who your last employer was, young lady, but my husband's rule was always a "fair wage for fair work". I'll pay you four and sixpence a week, with commission on any books you sell, on a month's trial. After that, we'll take a look at how you're getting on and take it from there. How's that?'

It was fine. Not quite as much as she'd earned as a lady's maid but she was confident that she would soon be earning more.

She smiled broadly and extended her right hand across the counter. 'It's a deal!'

She stayed until closing time and only left then because Mrs Liptrot insisted. It was so interesting. As she methodically examined the contents of the numerous bookshelves, she answered questions about her previous employment and how she had obtained her education and knowledge of books.

A number of customers came in, mainly businessmen and academics from the university but also a few ladies accompanied by their maid or husband, requiring books on wild flowers, garden birds and foreign travel. Mrs Liptrot directed her to the appropriate places on the shelves and then showed her how to enter the purchases and prices into the 'Sales' ledger and again in the 'Till' account – all to be balanced at the end of each day and the figures' total to be accurately balanced with the monetary total in the till.

Ellen loved every minute. She was going to enjoy this!

She soon fell into the routine of rising at 7.30 a.m., leaving the house at 8.00 a.m., a cup of strong tea on arrival, followed by opening the shop at 8.30 a.m. From then on, time was unnoticed. If there was an absence of customers, she used the time to familiarize herself with more of the stock or to pore over the accounts, checking the endless columns of figures in preparation for the annual auditors' inspection at the end of the year.

She found some of the top shelves to be in need of a good dusting and suggested moving some of the books to a more accessible place where they would catch the eye of likely buyers. Even more daringly, she suggested that some be displayed as 'bargain buys', with prices more suited to the pockets of some of the students at the Victoria University of Manchester, who quickly passed the word around that 'cheaper' books were to be obtained at Liptrot's Bookshop.

The weeks flew by. Ellen almost forgot about having to be careful in case she was spotted by Zach Durban on his travels. She was certain he never ventured into the more select area of town where the bookshop was situated and, as for entering such an establishment, he was more likely to fly to the moon.

So she was totally unprepared for the encounter one Saturday in mid-March when her way home was blocked by rows of uniformed policemen.

'What's happening, officer?' Ellen asked.

Recognizing her well-spoken tones, the officer replied, 'It's nothing to be alarmed at, miss. It's a "protest march" against low wages. If you stand here until they have all gone past, I'll see you safely on your way.'

Ellen did as she was bidden. She recognized, only too well, the grey pallor of undernourished bodies and the gaunt frames of men grown old too quickly.

Sullen looks were cast her way. To the casual eye, she seemed to have fared better than most. Her clothes were clean and in decent condition; her skin was a healthy tone; and her eyes sparkled clearly – unlike the condition of her observers. To the starving, grime-covered men who passed by, she seemed to be part of the over-privileged few.

She heard various remarks being tossed about. 'Rich folk!' 'Ne'er done a day's work!' 'Fancy clothes!' And, worse: 'Rich scum! Yah! We'll tread you under our feet!'

As faces scowled at her and fists were shaken, Ellen began to feel alarmed. Some of the men even spat in her direction, though none were near enough for the spittle to reach her.

'Keep your head down, miss,' the policeman warned.

Even as she heard his voice, Ellen felt her

heart go cold within her. The man who was just in front of them, mouthing obscenities, met her eyes with a mixture of loathing ... and a sudden twist of malicious delight.

It was Zach Durban.

The marchers swept him on his way but his venomous look chilled her whole body. He knew she was back.

Fourteen

'It was him, Grandma! I know it was. And he saw me. I saw the recognition in his eyes!'

Ellen was safely back at home, having been escorted there by one of the policemen. She was pacing up and down the front room, her skirt swishing at each turn.

Dorcas looked at her with some concern. 'If you're right, we'll have to be especially careful. I'll get a message to Ada to tell her to make sure that he doesn't follow her here. I don't think he knows where we live. You should be all right.'

Ellen shook her head. 'If I know Zach Durban, he'll have made it his business to know where you live!'

271

'Ask Mrs Liptrot if you can have a few days off work, Ellen. I'm sure she will allow it if you tell her there is someone you are frightened of.'

'She can't manage on her own. She needs me.'

'Then we'll ask Norman to accompany you to and from work. I'll take his place in the shop whilst he is with you.'

Norman agreed and their new routine began the next day, But Ellen knew she was going to have to find a more permanent solution or it wouldn't be safe for her to step outside.

After tossing a number of ideas around in her head for a few days, she knew her only course of action was to go away from the area. She didn't want to but she knew she would never be safe in Manchester while Zach Durban was likely to come looking for her. Where could she go? She couldn't look to their Tom for help, as she would if he lived anywhere but in Horwich. Where else could she go?

Did Charlie still think about her? Did he still remember the dreams they had shared? She doubted it. He wouldn't have stopped writing to her if he had hopes of a future together. She had held on to those hopes for too long. They were gone; shattered into oblivion.

A deep sadness almost took her breath away but she thrust it away. She had to get on with life. All her tomorrows were in her own hands. She must forget Charlie and make new decisions for her future, but she needed help to get started.

There was only one person she could turn to and that was John Oldfield. Would he still want to help her? He had said he would – but what if he had changed his mind? Would the shameful scene he had witnessed cloud his thoughts of her? The memory still made her feel defiled, shamed. Would John think the same? Was she now pushed away to some far corner of his mind; someone or something he didn't want to think about?

But, he had written to ask about her, hadn't he? Dared she take that chance?

She had to; there was no one else ... and it needn't be a permanent arrangement. Once she got established somewhere, she wouldn't hold him responsible for looking after her. All she needed was someone who could help her get far away from Zach Durban and then she would be able to plan her own future.

From the letter he had written to her grandma before Christmas, John intended to go back to Cambridge. Was he at the same lodgings? Would the landlady pass on a letter if he had moved? How would he respond?

There were so many uncertainties, she almost decided not to write – but her fear of Zach Durban urged her on. She was certain he was only biding his time; waiting until she felt safe – and then, he would pounce!

She told her mam what she was planning. Ada hugged her tightly. 'Oh, I've just got you back, Ellen. I don't want to lose you again. But you're right. You'll never be safe here. You've got to get away.'

So Ellen wrote the letter.

She didn't allow herself to brood about when a reply might arrive. The bookshop filled her days. Mrs Liptrot was allowing her more responsibility and she was thriving on it, regaining more confidence every day. But for the dark cloud of Zach Durban's potential threat, she would have been content to continue her life as it then was, but the threat was real.

'He's planning something,' her mam told her. 'He's gloating over it. Do take care.'

Ellen didn't need to be warned. She sometimes sensed someone was watching her as she and Norman made the twice-daily journey to and from the bookshop but she never caught sight of Zach Durban.

A few weeks passed by. She was beginning to think John no longer wanted to help her but then, as she arrived home from work one day in early June, she saw a letter propped up against an ornament on the top of the cabinet. She had paused in front of the mirror on the wall beyond the cabinet to pull the pins out of her hat and fluff up her hair where it had been flattened, but her hands stilled. The letter was addressed to her.

As she picked it up, her heart began to pound. 'It's from John Oldfield,' she said, staring at the envelope.

'Well, open it, then,' Dorcas urged.

Ellen slit open the envelope, her hands shaking as she pulled out the single piece of notepaper. She began to read and a rosy pink flush crept up her cheeks.

'He says my letter has only just been sent on to him. Oh, he's doing his final examinations and ... oh, my! He's coming to see me on Saturday! He's ... he's got a special question to ask me!'

John came, as promised. He travelled by train and hired a hansom cab outside Manchester's great railway station. The summer sky, laden with a pall of acrid smoke, was oppressive. How did people survive the summer here? How on earth had Ellen managed to rise from it?

A smile flickered over his face at the thought of her. Would she still be the same? He'd been so worried about her; desperate, even. When he first realized she had left the area, he hadn't known how to contact her; didn't know where she had gone; dreaded that she had been desperate enough to take her own life.

He had put notices in the Manchester newspapers and when he finally discovered her grandmother's address, he had written to her, but with no results. And then, her letter had arrived. How would she receive him? Her words had been friendly, but non-committal as far as her feelings were concerned. He glanced at his watch. Well, he'd know soon.

Had she been in touch with that farm boy? He hoped not. A slight pang twanged his conscience but he doused it immediately. He hadn't known where she was when Metcalfe had contacted him, had he? And he hadn't had the time to pass on this latest development. Besides, if Metcalfe really cared about Ellen, he'd have made his own inquiries. On top of that, 'all was fair in love and war', wasn't it? Or so he persuaded himself!

The cab was slowing down. John hastily readjusted his tie and cleared his throat. He'd arrived!

Ellen's grandmother opened the door to him. She was holding out her hand.

'Welcome, Mr Oldfield.'

He grasped her hand heartily. 'Good afternoon, Mrs Hilton. I've told the cab driver to return at 5.00 p.m. Is that all right?'

'Perfectly. Do come in.'

He removed his hat and followed her into the parlour. Ellen was standing across the room, looking as self-conscious as he felt. He halted in the doorway. He smiled but felt quite tongue-tied and all he could manage to say was, 'Hello.' How inadequate was that?

It didn't seem to matter. Ellen repeated his greeting, smiling hesitantly. He wanted to sweep her into his arms but social convention decreed otherwise and, after waiting for the two ladies to be seated, he perched on the edge of the padded upright chair to which he had been directed.

It was Dorcas who led the stilted conversation, ignoring the fact that his eyes were fixed on her granddaughter's face ... and Ellen's on his.

Although the questions barely registered in his mind, polite phrases rolled off his tongue, though he hardly knew what he said. 'Yes, thank you, I have had a very good journey.' 'Yes, Father and Mother are well – well, maybe not quite; Mother is still in convalescence.' 'Miss Sarah? Yes. In excellent health.' (Though she wasn't. Her hopes of marriage had been destroyed and she was still distraught beyond reason.) 'And you, Mrs Hilton? I hope you are well, also.'

There she was, seated demurely on a matching upright chair. Her hair was beautiful. It took his breath away. She had looped it up and piled it on top of her head but nothing could tame those curls. Bewitching tendrils escaped the confines of their restraint and tumbled over her forehead and in front of her ears. He longed to reach out a finger and let one of those locks curl around it, holding it prisoner. 'Pardon, Mrs Hilton? I'm afraid I didn't quite...Yes, Mrs Garland is still in charge of the kitchen ... and Nora? Yes ... she is. Goldie has gone ... but I don't know where. I haven't been home much, I'm afraid, since recovering from ... what happened.'

His inattention brought Dorcas's social conversation to a sudden stop. She rose to her feet and smoothed her hands down the front of her skirt. 'I must start preparations for the children's tea. If you will excuse me, I will...' The rest of her sentence was superfluous. Neither John nor Ellen was listening, though John had automatically risen to his feet when Dorcas rose, placing his china cup and saucer onto the small round table at his side. With a whispering rustle of her skirts, Dorcas glided from the room.

For a moment, neither moved. Ellen's lips were slightly parted. She felt as though her heart had stopped beating – but it hadn't. A fluttering in her chest confirmed it. Her left hand instinctively flew to that very area, her fingers spread wide.

He took a small step towards her.

Ellen rose from her seat in a fluid motion. Her eyes were level with his chin. She raised her eyelashes. 'John?' she whispered.

He took another step forward and gently placed his hands upon her shoulders. 'Ellen.' His voice sounded cracked, choked with emotion. 'I thought I would never see you again after that dreadful day. And when there was neither sight nor sound of you in all these months, I must admit, I feared you were dead, maybe lost on the moors.'

Her hands moved of their own volition, it

seemed. Her palms spread themselves against his chest. Even through his jacket, she could feel the rapid beating of his heart. If she laid her cheek against his chest, it would be a very comfortable place to be, of that she was certain. He hadn't yet declared the purpose of his visit, though the light in his eyes told her all she needed to know.

'I thought you were dead as well. There was so much blood.' Her voice sounded strange to her ears. 'I cried out to you not to die but I thought it was too late!'

'I know.' John took hold of her hands and raised them to his lips, gently caressing her fingers, whilst keeping his eyes upon hers. 'I think I heard you call my name. It seemed so far away and I struggled to reach you – but I had to let go.' His eyes searched her face for clues to her feelings. His heart leapt and began to beat faster again. 'It isn't too late, Ellen! We have another chance!'

Ellen felt her limbs tremble. John had held her like this before – and closer. She remembered his kisses last summer, when memories of Charlie had made her cut him short. With a surge of joy, she realized that her feelings for him weren't as dispassionate as she had feared. Her hands tingled as they rested in his and her lips longed for his to touch them. A smile lit her face but she lowered her eyes in shyness.

The action encouraged John to say more. He gently lifted her chin with a finger. 'I love you, Ellen. I have lain awake on my bed, dreaming of you and reliving every moment we spent together. I want you to become my wife. Can I hope?'

Ellen held her breath for a moment. It was her choice; her decision. A part of her heart still cried out to Charlie – but she forced it into submission. Charlie had forgotten her. It was John who held her in his arms. John who wanted to marry her.

John's eyes began to betray anxiety at her silence. 'Am I rushing you? I meant to approach this more slowly.' He smiled tenderly at her, causing her heart to miss a beat. 'I should have allowed you time to consider my proposal – but the sight of you, after all this time, made me want to swoop you up in my arms and whisk you away.'

Ellen laughed delightedly and shook her head at his misgivings. 'Yes, John.'

John looked startled, almost as if he didn't understand her simple reply. 'Yes? You said yes?' He was about to pull her into his arms, when he paused. 'Is that, Yes, I have reason to hope? Or, Yes, you'll become my wife?

Or...' His voice almost faded away. 'Or, Yes, I have rushed you too fast?'

Ellen's eyes twinkled at his dilemma. 'It's, yes, I'll become your wife.'

'You will? Hurrah!' With that loud shout, he put his hands around her slim waist and swung her round. He gently lowered her back to her feet, his eyes fixed on her face, smiling at what he saw there. With a contented sigh, he drew her towards him and gently placed his lips upon hers.

Her ready response stimulated his ardour and, for a moment, they were lost in the wonder of discovering the feel and taste of each other. As they drew apart, John became serious. He traced his fingers gently over the contours of her face, as if to memorize them forever. 'There's a lot for us to do. We'll tell your grandmother first, and then I need to see about getting home to let my father know.'

'Will he be angry?'

John hesitated. 'I don't know. I told him that I was coming here to ask you. He wasn't best pleased, but he knew that I wouldn't change my mind. His only hope was that you would refuse.' He kissed her again. 'But it's too late to change your mind now. I have claimed you with my kisses.' He took hold of both her hands. 'Come on. Let's ask your grandmother for her blessing.'

Dorcas's eyes sparkled as she saw the happiness reflected in their faces and in the joyful looks they constantly exchanged and she readily gave her blessing.

'Are you considering a long engagement?'

They looked at each other. 'We haven't discussed it,' John admitted, 'but from what Ellen told me in her letter, I think the sooner the better, don't you? Your stepfather's not been round here bothering you, has he?'

'Not yet, but I don't trust him to stay away forever. He's just biding his time.'

John did rapid calculations. 'I can be back here by Monday or Tuesday. If I get a special licence, we could be married on Wednesday – or do you think you would be better coming away with me now? We could marry before I tell my father, if you wish.'

Ellen's heart and head were in conflict. She was desperate to get away from the danger Zach Durban presented, but felt she needed time to tell her family goodbye. Her mother would be distraught if she were to lose her again without the chance to say a proper farewell.

Dorcas Hilton understood her granddaughter's dilemma. She quietly offered her advice. 'Go back to your father, Mr Oldfield and tell him of your intentions. We'll make our arrangements here and I think, if you agree, that next Saturday will be soon enough for your wedding.'

After John departed, Ellen and Dorcas began to plan what needed to be done.

'What shall I wear? I can't get married in my work frock!'

Dorcas smiled. 'When you told me John Oldfield was coming to see you, I suspected this happy outcome and I bought a length of dark-red lightweight wool-tweed from the market, my dear. It will make an excellent dress for both your wedding and travelling. And I bought a pattern that won't be too difficult to make up. Come upstairs and let me show it to you.'

Ellen followed her grandma up the stairs to her room, where Dorcas opened her wardrobe and removed a parcel from the lower shelf. She laid it on her bed and removed the wrapping paper. 'There, what do you think?'

Ellen felt tears spring to her eyes. 'Oh, Grandma! I do love you! It will be perfect, I just know it!'

'We'll start on it this evening after we've got the children to bed. I'm sure Lizzie will help, too. She has a neat hand for stitching, just as you have.'

When Lizzie returned, bringing home the children, she wanted to be told everything. Flossie, Maud and the children were equally excited. They remembered Lizzie and Norman's wedding and delighted in the prospect of another. The younger ones jumped up and down in their excitement.

'Can we be bridesmaids? And have a new frock?' Flossie wanted to know.

'There mightn't be time,' Ellen warned. 'We've only got six days and we can't afford a grand affair. It'll have to be in the registry office.'

Flossie pouted. 'It's not fair. You never think of anyone but yourself!'

'That's quite enough, Flossie!' Dorcas said sharply. 'You have already had new clothes since Ellen came home. You must wait a few months before I can buy more material. And don't scowl like that! The wind might change and you will look like that forever!'

Flossie flounced out of the room, still muttering about how unfair it was. The other children continued to jump about in excitement. Any excuse for a special tea could only be good news!

It was a busy week. Ellen wouldn't have

thought it possible to get everything done in such a short time but Dorcas was a born planner and supervisor.

She measured Ellen against the paper pattern and made the necessary adjustments. Ellen held her breath when Dorcas began to cut the material. All her other clothes had been bought second-hand or were cut-downs of Miss Sarah's. This dress would be her very own!

It was made into a double-breasted tailored suit with long tight sleeves and shaped velvet cuffs that matched the collar, the buttons and the hem of the long flared skirt. Underneath, she was to wear a white cotton shirt with a high-stand collar and a brooch that Dorcas found amongst her few pieces of jewellery.

'I'll ask Mrs Thornham next door if she'll trim a plain hat with some of the velvet,' Dorcas promised. 'She used to work for a milliner and is happy to oblige folk. And then you, my dear, will be a bride to be proud of.'

The week of frenzied activity sped by. Some close neighbours offered to make some cakes and pies, jellies and custards for the wedding breakfast and Dorcas made the finest cake she could afford.

Telling Mrs Liptrot of her impending departure was hard to do. They had discussed plans for future improvements to the business but Mrs Liptrot agreed that Ellen's safety was of greater importance. 'I wish you well, my dear, but our customers will miss you.'

Friday dawned with a clear blue sky. The finishing touches were put to her wedding outfit and Dorcas hung it on the back of the living room door. 'I'll take it upstairs later,' she promised. 'Now, there's just your hat to get. I'll pop round to see if Mrs Thornham has finished it.'

She went next door, leaving Ellen to brush up the loose threads and snippets of fabric that littered the floor. A sense of excitement was building in her; John would be here soon. He might even be in Manchester now. She must get her outfit upstairs before he came; he mustn't see it before tomorrow! Now, there were just those scraps of material over there

Hearing the latch click and the back door open, she called out, 'Did you forget something?'

'Nothing I can't put right!'

Her blood ran cold: it was Zach Durban.

The brush and dustpan fell from her hand as she leapt to her feet and faced the man of her nightmares. His face was unshaven, his greasy hair unbrushed and his clothes dirty. The reeking smell of alcohol and stale body odour wafted across the space between them. Slapping a doubled-over belt in the palm of his left hand, he moved forward.

Ellen dodged round the kitchen table, making it a barrier between them. She was afraid. 'What are you doing here?' she demanded harshly. 'Get out! Grandma's only next door! She'll hear!' She wished she were at the other side of the room; she could have banged on the wall.

'Surely I can come and visit me own daughter on th'eve of her wedding?' His voice whined, as though he was penitent for his past behaviour – but the cold gleam in his bloodshot eyes belied his words.

'You're not my father, I'm glad to say,' Ellen retorted. 'I left your clutches when I went to Horwich ten years ago. Do you think I haven't told people what you did to me? I'm not a little girl now – so get out of here before I call for help.'

'Huh! Miss High and Mighty! Well, I've heard about what yer've been getting up to, up yonder. And you dare to tell your lies about me! You've been nothing but trouble ever since the day I clapped eyes on you. An' yer mam's no better – two bastards to her name. She didn't deserve a fellow like me. Took you on as me own, I did, yer ungrateful wretch!'

He lurched towards her and Ellen backed away. If she could just keep out of his reach and slowly circle around until she was nearer the door...

A sudden flick of his hand sent an upright wooden chair skittering across the room. The sight of her wedding outfit hanging on the back of the living room door seemed to enrage him further and, with one lunge of his arm, he pulled it off the back of the door and trampled it under his feet. His eyes gloated with malice, satisfied by Ellen's cry of distress.

Another swift movement of his arm sent the kitchen table out of his way and he lashed forwards with his folded belt. Ellen ducked and whirled aside. Zach lunged after her but she was more agile than he and evaded his clutches. He snorted like an enraged bull, his neck bulging out from his dirty necktie, his spittle flecked on the stubble of his chin.

The stench of his breath made her stomach heave. She glanced around in desperation, looking for some sort of weapon to fend him off with. The poker lay in the hearth. As she dodged yet another swing of the belt, she lunged down and snatched it up.

Zach laughed in derision. 'What d'you think you'll do with that?' he taunted. 'Get near enough to hit me and I'll have yer first wi' me belt. Come on! Come an' try it!'

He lowered his arm, daring her to step closer.

Ellen wouldn't be drawn. She would bide her time, confident that she could out-manoeuvre him. But, unprepared for the ingenuity he had learned in his ringside seat at the prize fights, she was wrong-footed as he feigned a right lunge that quickly became a left grab at her hair. She screamed as he twisted it around in his hand, pulling her close, his breath steaming into her face.

'Now I'll show yer! You'll regret the day you ever crossed swords wi' me.'

All the horror of the abuse in her child-hood and more recently at Leslie Fairchild's hands welled up within her. Her hand hold-ing the poker was trapped between their bodies and she had to let it fall, but her left hand, fingers outspread like talons, tore across his face leaving four parallel red weals, soon weeping red droplets.

The flow of obscenities that poured from his mouth enraged her more. She knew that if he flung her from him, she would be at the mercy of his powerful strength and the belt would cut her flesh to ribbons. Screaming wildly, she grabbed at his arm and kicked at his shins. Her hair was screwed round in his hand right to the roots. The pain was excruciating.

A movement behind him caught her eye. Someone had come to help her!

Zach saw the flicker of her eyes. 'You don't catch me wi' that old one,' he snarled ... just as his wife swung the heavy iron shovel at his head. His face froze in disbelief as he dropped forwards to the floor quicker than a swatted fly. The weight of his body took Ellen down with him and she lay stunned, partly trapped beneath him.

Ada helped to release her and she scrambled to her feet, clinging to her mother for a moment's relief. Her breath hurt her throat as she sought to control the rasping sobs. 'Mam! Oh, Mam!'

Ada's silence and rigid stance puzzled her.

'Mam?' She drew back and stared at her. Ada's hands covered her mouth.

Ellen followed her mam's shocked expression. Her stepfather was lying still and silent. His blank, staring eyes would never lust after her or anyone else again.

'Oh, Mam! What've we done!'

The shovel fell from Ada's limp hand, clanging on the stone-flagged floor. 'Oh, Lord! I've killed him! I've murdered my own husband! They'll hang me, for sure!' Her hands were pressed against the sides of her face, now white with terror.

Ellen's hand flew to her mouth. 'What can we do?' she whispered.

Ada sank to her knees. 'I didn't mean to kill him – but I couldn't stand by and see him beat you like that. I knew he was coming 'ere. I've had our Herbie following him. I knew, as soon as he ran back to tell me which way he was going.' She dropped her head into her hands. 'What'll I do?'

A loud knocking at the front door startled them.

'Don't answer it!' Ada said sharply, her eyes fearful.

The knock was repeated.

Ellen patted her mam's shoulder. 'I'll see who it is. Stay quiet.'

She left the kitchen, carefully closing the door behind her, wishing she could shut out the scene in the kitchen permanently.

Whoever their visitor was knocked again. Ellen opened the front door tentatively, prepared to tell whoever it was to come back later – but it was John.

She fell into his arms, sobbing onto his shoulder.

John eased her back inside, closing the door behind him. Her dishevelled state appalled him. What on earth had happened?

Wordlessly, Ellen drew him across the living room and into the kitchen. He saw the broken chair; the table cloth pulled to the floor, with broken crockery upon it; and a white-faced woman, her hands wringing in fear. 'What on earth's happened?' He suddenly saw the man slumped on the floor behind the woman, his eyes wide and staring. He looked back at Ellen. 'Who's that? Is that your stepfather?'

Before they could answer, another voice broke upon their ears. 'Ellen! What's been going on?' Dorcas stood in the doorway, her face strained and anxious. 'I heard such a noise. What...?'

She saw the still body sprawled across her kitchen floor. 'Zach Durban!' Her hands covered her white cheeks. 'Is he dead?'

In disjointed phrases Ellen and Ada told them both what had happened.

'I'd better call at the police station and tell them to get someone round here,' John suggested, when they had finished.

'No!' Ada cried. 'What if they don't believe us? I've killed 'im! They'll send me to prison. I know they will! They'll hang me!' She was trembling. 'Don't give me up, our Ellen. I couldn't face it!'

Ellen set her face in firm resolve. 'No, I won't! I'm not having you blamed for this. He had it coming to him – but we need to think quickly. Where should he be right now?'

Ada controlled her shaking body. 'I don't know ... anywhere ... in bed ... in the ale-house ... watching a fight ... in a fight. Since he's been out o' work, he's been makin' trouble all over the place.'

Dorcas's mind sprang into action. Like the others, she was shocked but spared no pity for the man. 'Thank goodness Mrs Thornham is as deaf as a doorpost! We need to get a wheelbarrow from somewhere. It's the only way we'll manage to shift him.' She looked at Ada, weighing up if she was capable of helping with the disposal of Zach's body.

Ada anticipated her question. 'I'm all right, Mam. I stopped carin' for 'im years ago. I just feel shock at the way it's 'appened. I'll be all right. Just let me get meself together.'

'We'll have to get him into the woodshed for now,' Dorcas decided. 'The children won't see him there. We can put the padlock on the door. Come on, quickly now. Lizzie will be back soon ... and Flossie, too.'

That evening and the following day passed in a blur.

Once Zach Durban's body was locked in the woodshed and the kitchen furniture put to rights, Dorcas hustled John and Ellen off to stay in the hotel where John had booked a room for himself.

'Tidy yourself up, Ellen,' she urged, 'and take your wedding outfit. You'll be able to sponge the marks off and get a maid to press it for you. I'll make any necessary excuses for the slight change of plans here and John will take care of everything else, won't you?'

'Of course. And I'll come back after dark to remove the body.'

Which he did.

It was a strange eve of her wedding, Ellen mused after John had settled her into a room and asked for her meal to be served there.

He had been loath to leave her but Ellen had assured him she was all right.

That man's death was not going to spoil the rest of her life! She would cope. She had to. Her mam's life depended on her keeping

calm and acting as though nothing un-
toward had happened. 'I'll see you tomorrow at the registry office,' she said as she bid
John goodnight.

'That's my girl! And by this time tomorrow, we will be Mr and Mrs John Oldfield!'

Fifteen

Ellen leaned back against the seat and let the
regular rhythm of the train take over her
consciousness for a few moments. Two weeks
had passed since their wedding and they were
on their way back to Horwich. However, it
hadn't been the blissful honeymoon they had
both hoped for. How could it, with memories
of Zach Durban and Leslie Fairchild
resurging at unbidden moments?

Memories of her stepfather were the easiest
to evade. Their horror stemmed from the
past: he had deserved his fate. A carefully
worded letter from Dorcas, including
newspaper cuttings reporting the death, had
set their minds at ease that there would be no
repercussions awaiting them on their return.
The man who first stumbled on Zach's body

in the early hours of Ellen's and John's wedding day reported the death to the police. Ada had played the part of the shocked widow and the rest of the family rallied round to support her.

Zach's reputation and the scratches down his face had set the police searching the 'red light' district but their inquiries had been inconclusive. He had been in a fight with persons unknown. His head had been cracked by his fall. Overnight rain had washed away any evidence to the contrary.

It was Leslie Fairchild's assault that was harder for Ellen to evade. John had witnessed her shame. He had seen her being defiled. He said he had put it from his memory, but could she believe him? It hadn't gone from her memory. She had thought she could overcome it but, as she prepared for bed each night, the flashbacks returned.

She tried to focus her mind on John and his obvious love for her ... and John tried to be patient and understanding. They both pretended the other had succeeded but it lay like a barrier between them. John hadn't expected it to be easy. What he wanted to do out of love for her had already violated her innocence. He could see it in her eyes, though she tried to hide it and he felt it in the rigidity of her body when the light was turned out and he held her in his arms.

In the daytime, they became friends again and enjoyed the delights of the seaside. The weather was kind and they strolled along the promenade, played croquet and sat in tea gardens listening to the brass band playing.

Their marriage was consummated on their fourth night together. John was gentle and Ellen was passive. Neither spoke. John held her in his arms afterwards and murmured tender words against her hair and Ellen snuggled against him. It hadn't been so bad ... and it would get better, she knew it would.

'What are you thinking?' John now asked, smiling as he gazed down at her. He gently stroked her cheeks with the back of his fingers. Tendrils of her hair had sprung free of the clips and framed her face. He let one of them curl round his finger, taking the opportunity to kiss her cheek. His heart still seemed bent on stopping every time he touched her.

Ellen opened her eyes. 'I was remembering some of the lovely days we've had in the past two weeks.'

John kissed her lips, thankful that they were alone in the railway carriage and could dispense with social propriety. Ellen responded, allowing the sweet sensations, build within her, marvelling that she was beginning to enjoy close intimacy. If only they could remain in this small cocoon of love for each other.

John slipped his arm around her shoulders and drew her against his chest. 'I love you more each day,' he murmured into her hair. 'You won't let my parents distress you, will you?'

The reminder of the purpose of their return to Horwich drove away Ellen's composure. Her heart fluttered fearfully. The lives of the whole household had been torn apart by Leslie Fairchild's attack on her. The intervening months hadn't lessened its impact. John marrying her would be like rubbing salt into a wound ... painful to bear, especially for his mother.

'I'm not looking forward to seeing them, I must admit, but I will stand by your side as you try to become reconciled with them.'

John hesitated, aware that this visit wouldn't be easy, but Ellen was now his wife. His family must be made aware that he wasn't ashamed of her. 'I won't leave you alone with them. If we can't stay in the house, we'll book in at one of the hotels for a few days. I need to discuss the details of my master's degree course with Mr Howard at the Loco Works before we go back to Cambridge.'

Ellen wondered, not for the first time, if they were being over-optimistic in thinking that she and John could return to Horwich when he finished his master's. But that was a year away. It was today's ordeal she should be thinking about – returning now, so that John could introduce her as his wife to his parents. She would have preferred to leave it with the letter he had sent from Eastbourne and gone straight to Cambridge to stay in some digs John had secured, but John had seen that as the coward's way out. He had insisted that this was the right thing to do and besides, he needed some of his personal possessions. He was confident that, now it was a fait accompli, as he put it, his parents would accept their marriage. Ellen didn't share his optimism.

'Look, we're nearly there.' John's voice interrupted her sombre thoughts.

Rivington Pike stood proudly on the skyline with the Rivington moors and Winter Hill stretching eastwards. Ellen's breath caught in her throat. She loved that skyline view. She loved Horwich. She had loved being able to walk up George's Lane to escape the smoke pollution of the town and breathe the sharp fresh air of the moors.

Maybe it would work out all right?

She was quiet as the cab took them from the station to Chapel Lane. She knew every turn of the road, every house, almost every tree, but this was the first time she had driven along here as Mrs John Oldfield and, although the name still gave her a thrill every time she let her mind dwell on it, right now, all she felt was dread.

It wasn't going to be easy to step back inside that house. It was only her love for John that had brought her this far. Even her fellow servants would disapprove of her rise in status.

John patted her hand and smiled encouragingly at her. 'They won't bite,' he assured her.

'No, but they might try,' Ellen replied. 'Even without ... what happened ... they won't exactly be overjoyed.'

'Whatever we face, we face it together,' John reminded her, 'so, come on. We're here. Let's face the lions in their den.'

He helped her out of the cab and turned to speak to the driver, who had moved towards the luggage, strapped on at the back. 'Leave it there, for now. I'll come back out

301

for it when I know what we're doing.'

He stood for a moment, looking up at the house that had been his home all his life. There was no one ready to welcome them, though he had cabled their expected time of arrival. His departure had been marred by his mother's screams of rage at her son's refusal to break off his 'so-called' engagement. It had been a lot worse than he had portrayed to Ellen. Even his father had been cold with anger and his sister had shut herself in her room, crying hysterically. He doubted that the intervening weeks had done much to soothe them but hoped that their 'breeding', of which his mother was so proud, would, at the very least, persuade them to be polite to his bride.

Hand in hand, they went up the few steps. John put his key into the lock but it didn't fit. Puzzled, he withdrew the key and looked at it. It seemed to be in order. He tried again without success. 'They've changed the lock,' he said to Ellen. 'Not to worry.' He gave the bell pull a tug.

Ellen could imagine the sound of the jangling tones of the bell in the kitchen as it alerted the downstairs staff that their attention was required. It seemed an age before they could hear the sound of someone coming, probably Bert Cadman.

John smiled reassuringly at Ellen, holding her tightly around her waist with his left hand. She nestled in towards him, thankful of his support.

The door opened. Contrasting expressions fled across Bert's face as his glance passed swiftly over them. His first look of polite inquiry quickly changed to recognition of his master's son and, just as quickly, the shutters came down as he enacted his master's orders. 'I'm sorry, Mr John. Your father isn't at home.'

'Come off it, Cadman,' John replied. 'You can't put me off with that one. He knows we are coming and he didn't tell me not to.' He made as if to push past the man but was firmly prevented.

'I'm sorry, sir, but I have my orders. I can't let you in, not with ... your wife.' He glanced apologetically towards Ellen. 'I'm sorry, Harris ... miss ... missus,' his usual bland demeanour slipping slightly.

Ellen knew her cheeks were burning. She turned towards John in mute appeal, her eyes pleading. They shouldn't have come. Not yet. It was too soon. 'John?'

John refused to be that readily dissuaded. This was his wife who was being insulted and, however much he respected his parents, especially his father, Ellen now came first in his life. He tightened his grip around her shoulders. 'Go and tell my father that we're here, Cadman, and that he must come and tell me himself that he won't let us into his house.'

Cadman kept his features neutral. 'I'm sorry, sir. The master was most definite.' He glanced quickly over his shoulder and lowered his voice. 'The mistress, your mother, isn't well enough. Maybe you should try on your own, sir – or at the works later on. I believe the master will be there later this afternoon.'

John drew himself up. 'Tell my father that we called,' he said stiffly, 'and that we will be staying at the Crown Hotel. He may contact us there, if he wishes. Good day.' He tipped his hat and drew Ellen down the steps with as much dignity as he could muster. He held open the door of the cab for her and followed her inside without a backward glance. 'The Crown Hotel,' he crisply ordered the driver.

As the afternoon wore on, Ellen's nerves were as taut as a wire used to cut a wedge of cheese. Mr Oldfield senior hadn't yet made an appearance and John was pacing ceaselessly up and down the carpet in their room in the Crown Hotel.

It was a room at the front of the hotel and overlooked Scholes Bank. Ellen longed to be out in the sunshine, maybe to go for a stroll through Lever Park towards Rivington or down to Anderton Bridge and along Jepson's Clough to the River Douglas and stroll along its banks, but she knew there was no point in suggesting it. John was so certain his father would come.

She did her best to maintain a cheerful conversation, only to hear John snap, 'Is there nothing you can be doing, Ellen? My head is bouncing with the sound of your voice!'

She knew it was because he was as much on edge as she was, probably more so, but it hurt to be the butt of his annoyance.

'Shall I order afternoon tea?' she suggested timidly.

'As you please.'

A maid wheeled in a small trolley loaded with a pot of tea and a two-tiered cake stand with slices of cakes and pastries, but John couldn't settle. His fingers crumpled the slice of coffee and walnut cake to pieces and after two or three sips of his tea, he was once more pacing the carpet.

Ellen sighed. She felt no better herself

and, although it looked delicious, the cake tasted as dry as dust in her mouth.

At seven o'clock that evening, John realized his father wasn't coming.

'Get changed,' he said brusquely. 'We'll go down to dinner.'

At least, in the dining room, John's social etiquette compelled him to make an effort to be sociable and Ellen tried to keep cheerful, but found it difficult to maintain. She bit back many an apology that sprang to her lips and was thankful when the evening drew to its close and they made their way upstairs to the privacy of their room.

At first, they lay stiffly side by side but shortly after Ellen snuggled against him and laid her arm across his chest, John turned towards her. He nestled his head against her breast and Ellen stroked his skin and murmured words of love. It was the first time she had taken any initiative in their love-making and she was pleased when she sensed John's ardour arise.

He took her quite forcefully but Ellen tried not to mind. She knew he was hurting and didn't mean to treat her so harshly. Afterwards, they lay in each other's arms, finding comfort in their closeness. She snuggled closer to him, longing for the gentleness he had shown in their previous love-making.

Eventually, John murmured, 'I'm sorry, love. I've been a brute, haven't I?'

'You have a bit,' she agreed. She nuzzled against his chest and ran her hand slowly along the length of his body. 'Do you want to make amends?' she purred softly.

He raised himself up on one elbow and leaned over her, his free hand caressing her face, her hair, her breasts. A slow smile spread over his face. 'Ellen Oldfield, I do believe there's a bit of a wanton woman hiding away in you ... who is longing to come out and show herself.'

He gently lowered his head and covered her lips with his. This time, their love-making was sweet and lovely ... and stirred emotions deep within her that seemed to spiral around, taking her to the brink of something so wonderful that she was filled with a sense of deep expectancy ... for she knew that, whatever that wonderful something was, it would change her forever.

But, she didn't quite get there.

Not that she told John, of course. How could she? She knew he had found it. He cried her name in exhilaration as he reached the peak of his passion, his face rapt with wonder. But, for now, she was satisfied to have given such joy to him – because he loved her.

Still glowing with the memory of their shared love, they faced the next day with renewed hope of reconciliation with John's parents – or, at least, with his father.

'I really do think that you should go to see him at the works,' Ellen declared, when he hadn't been in touch with them by lunchtime. 'We can't go away, without any contact at all.' She looked steadily into his eyes. 'We're the ones who have broken the unwritten code, so it's up to us to make the moves back. If he won't receive you there, then at least you will know that you tried.'

John reluctantly agreed to this proposal. 'What will you do whilst I'm gone?'

'I would like to go to the Lower Barn at Rivington and walk by the reservoir. It was one of my favourite places.'

'Well, take a cab. I'll order one at the desk for you. Come on. We may as well leave together.'

The peace by the reservoir was just as she re-membered it. The blue of the sky was re-flected in the calm water, invoking memories of the past. But it was being here with Charlie that invaded her mind, not John. A pain stabbed at her heart. Maybe she shouldn't have come – not to this particular place. She took a deep breath. Charlie was in the past. John deserved better.

Sensing that time was passing, she knew she must make her way back to the old tithe barn where her cab was waiting. She turned ... and her heart skipped a beat. A young man was striding towards her. He stopped ... and so did she. Her lips formed his name, though no sound came.

It was Charlie!

Oh, Charlie! Why have you come? Had her thoughts about him conjured up an apparition? No, he was real enough. Her face blanched as he came towards her, dreading, yet longing for physical contact with him. Her lips, her arms, her whole body cried out for his touch.

He stopped a few yards away from her, his face taut like her own. They faced each other, without speaking, a myriad of thoughts tormenting and hurting, rioting through their minds.

It was Charlie who broke the silence. 'I believe congratulations are in order.' His voice lacked any emotion and tore through her heart like a blade of cold steel.

'Yes,' she whispered, glancing down at her left hand, where her wedding ring shone, partnered by her engagement ring. 'How did you know where to find me?'

'I saw Doris in town. She told me you had called at the house yesterday and that you were staying at the Crown, so I called in there and they said you had come here. I wanted to see for myself.'

Ellen looked at him, her mind crying out his name and the question, 'Why?' The last word slipped from her lips, unbidden. 'Why, Charlie? Why did you stop writing to me?'

Charlie shot her a surprised look. 'Me? I didn't. But your letters got fewer and fewer until they stopped altogether!'

'No. You stopped writing to me.'

Why was he lying? Why didn't he just tell her? If he'd met someone else, she'd understand. She'd try to. A sob arose in her throat. Why had she come?

'You didn't answer my letters,' she cried. 'I thought you had stopped loving me.'

He shook his head. 'I didn't stop writing. I loved you, Ellen. I was distraught when they said you had gone and no one knew where you were.'

He made a gesture as though to take hold of her hands but pulled back. 'I had to go

310

back to Birmingham but I kept coming home, hoping to hear something,' he continued. 'I saw John a few weeks later. He said he didn't know where you'd gone, either.'

Ellen shook her head, frantically trying to put together the broken pieces of conflicting words. 'No! I wrote and wrote – six times to every one of yours. Then they started coming back to me. You'd gone – and I didn't know where!'

'I wrote to tell you I had to change my digs. I did! I can't remember how many times! You didn't reply. It wasn't me who stopped writing! It was you!'

Ellen shook her head. 'I didn't get them!'

This couldn't be happening!

She thought of the days when she had longed for the postman to bring her Charlie's letters – and the dreadful days ... weeks ... when none came. Until she had stopped expecting them. The disappointment ... the hurting ... the despair.

'You even stopped writing to Goldie,' she accused, defending her position.

Now it was Charlie's turn to shake his head. 'Goldie? What are you talking about? I only wrote to Goldie once, to ask her if you were ill ... or if something had happened to you. She didn't reply.'

Ellen remembered Goldie taunting her with letters in Charlie's handwriting. He had to be lying. 'Goldie had lots of letters from you. She used to wave them in my face. You wrote more to her than you did to me.'

'No, I didn't,' Charlie insisted. 'I know I didn't write as often as you did. I was too tired. I was working long hours so that I could save up enough money for us to be married. It was your letters that stopped coming. I came home as soon as I could ... after I found out what had happened – but I was too late. You'd gone!'

He made a move towards her but Ellen stepped back. Her body longed for his embrace, remembered the ecstasy of his kisses, yearned to be held by him – but she knew she couldn't let him. With his arms around her, she would believe his excuses and forgive him the hurt. Her resolve to resist him would be too weak. She mustn't let him hold her – not even in her thoughts. Her lips still tingled with the memory of his kisses. Why couldn't they forget him ... as she was forcing her mind to forget? Why did her body still ache for his touch? It was like a severe pain; low in her abdomen. She almost cried out with the severity of it – only she mustn't let him know. No one must know! John mustn't know … not ever!

Realizing Charlie was still speaking, Ellen tried to pull her thoughts together.

'Then my boss asked me to go to America to look at the motor assembly lines over there,' he was saying. 'I agreed. I thought it would help me get over you … but it didn't. I just got back last week.'

Ellen stared at him, trying to sort out the jumble of thoughts. He had to be lying. It didn't make sense.

Charlie impulsively took hold of her hands. 'Ellen, come away with me. We'll go away where nobody knows us. I still love you. I will always love you – and I know you love me. I can see it in your eyes. Nothing will change that! You can't possibly love John Oldfield like you love me. He'll get over you. I can't bear life without you, knowing that someone else holds you in his arms.'

The mention of John's name brought Ellen back to her senses with a jolt. She pulled away from him, stepping backwards out of his reach.

'No, I can't. I can't do that to him … I do love him… I wouldn't have married him if I didn't! He must never know. I'm sorry, Charlie! I'm sorry!'

Her voice faltered and faded away. She

313

looked at him in anguished despair. 'I must go. No, don't try to stop me. It's too late. We've found each other again too late.'

With a broken sob, she tore away from him and ran to the road, where her cab was waiting, leaving Charlie staring disconsolately after her.

It was late afternoon when Ellen arrived back at the hotel, relieved that she was back before John.

She sank onto the bed and let her anguish sob out of her. 'Oh, Charlie! John!' However would she manage? If only she had waited! But, no! She mustn't think that! She mustn't! She loved John ... she did! She couldn't bear to hurt him. He had given up his family for her. She buried her face in her hands, overcome by her distress.

She must forget Charlie. John deserved a faithful wife and that is what she would be. Whatever happened between John and his father today, they would face it together.

Her firm resolve strengthened her. She slipped along to the bathroom and washed her face in cold water. Then she peered at her reflection in the mirror. She looked dreadful.

She returned to their room and stared disconsolately out of the window, not seeing the passing traffic or pedestrians. She didn't know how long she stood there.

A knock at the door drew her attention.

'Come in!'

The porter stood in the doorway, his face inscrutable. 'There is a person to see you, Mrs Oldfield. That is, if you wish to see her.' His voice expressed doubt that she would but, as he stepped back slightly, a smaller figure became evident.

Ellen stared ... then a slow smile spread across her face and she held out her hands. 'Doris! It's you! Oh, how lovely of you to come! Come in!'

Doris looked ill at ease but she entered the room. 'I wasn't sure I ought to come,' she said, 'but I thought you might like these.' She thrust a package forward. It was bundled untidily together, wrapped in brown paper and held together with much-knotted string.

'What is it?' Ellen asked curiously, taking the package and turning it round in her hands.

'Goldie left it ... when she left. She said she didn't mean to hurt you like that. She was having a baby. Did you know?'

Ellen shook her head. 'No, I didn't know. Poor Goldie. Who was the father? Did she say?' She was still curious about the package in her hands.

'She said it was Mr Fairchild ... but he had already been sent packing after ... after what happened to you. There was an awful to-do about it. Miss Sarah was made real poorly and Mrs Oldfield quite lost her wits for a while!' Doris sounded uncomfortable and added, 'I'm not supposed to say.'

'It's all right, Doris. I understand. John said as much.' She supposed she had been fortunate not to be put in the same condition. She was unsure whether to open the package now, or to wait until Doris had gone. What would Goldie have left for her?

Doris was already backing towards the door. 'I'd best go, Ellen ... Mrs Oldfield, I mean.'

'Yes. Thank you for coming, Doris. We ... we had some good times, didn't we?'

Doris looked doubtful. 'I suppose so. It's different now, though.'

When Doris had gone, Ellen sat on the edge of the bed and began to undo the knots that held the parcel together. The knots resisted her first efforts but she eventually had the better of them.

The brown paper fell open to reveal an assortment of letters, some addressed to her in Charlie's handwriting and some of her letters to Charlie – letters she thought had been posted.

She picked them up, one by one, staring at them. Some had been opened; others were still sealed. Her hands fell limply into her lap, the last letter slipping from her grasp. Her cheeks felt drained of colour and strength.

How long she sat there, Ellen never knew. Her mind was paralysed, her body numb. 'Oh, Goldie! Why?' What had she ever done to Goldie to make her do this?

It was the sound of people's voices out in the corridor that brought her back to reality. She looked at the letters fanned out on the bed in front of her. They held all her love of yesteryear, all her hopes and all her dreams for a better 'tomorrow' – a tomorrow with Charlie.

Charlie hadn't lied; he hadn't stopped writing to her; he hadn't stopped loving her. He was as much a victim as she was ... and so was John.

More voices sounded outside the door. She heard John speak to someone. The doorknob rattled, then stopped, as she heard a man's voice reply.

Quickly, she scooped up all the letters and pushed them back into the brown paper wrap. Where could she put them until she could dispose of them?

Their luggage was stacked neatly by the door, ready to be carried downstairs. Ellen hurriedly pushed the letters into her personal bag. She would destroy them as soon as she could. They were part of the past. No one can live properly wrapped up in the past. Neither can anyone change it. 'What's done is done', her grandma often used to say. The future was ahead of them – hers and John's. That was where her hopes now lay. She wouldn't even read the letters. It would hurt too much. The doorknob rattled again and John entered to greet her with a kiss.

'He wouldn't see me,' he said shortly. 'We may as well go. There's a train to Bolton in half an hour. Let's get on our way back. The porter is here to take our trunks to the cab outside. Are you ready?'

Ellen forced the events of the past couple of hours out of her mind as she tilted her face up towards him.

'Yes, love. I'm ready.'

The publishers hope that this book has given you enjoyable reading. Large Print Books are especially designed to be as easy to see and hold as possible. If you wish a complete list of our books please ask at your local library or write directly to:

Magna Large Print Books
Magna House, Long Preston,
Skipton, North Yorkshire.
BD23 4ND